The Princess
of Cortova

The
Princess of Cortova

Diane Stanley

HARPER
An Imprint of HarperCollinsPublishers

ISBN 978-0-06-204730-4

Typography by Adam B. Bohannon

13 14 15 16 17   CG/RRDH   10 9 8 7 6 5 4 3 2 1

❖

First Edition

for my darlin' Clementine

CONTENTS

Part One

Chess—a strategic board game for two players in
which the pieces are moved across a checkered
board according to precise rules, which differ
for each type of piece. The object of the game is
to force the opposing king into a position from which
there can be no escape (*checkmate*).

Opening—the beginning phase of a game.

Day One

❦ 1 ❧

The Summer Palace

PELENOS, THE GREAT ROYAL city of Cortova, was a pesthole in summer. As the punishing sun baked its cobbles and walls, the air grew thick with sewer-stench. The poor slept out on rooftops and porches at night, hoping to catch a breeze; by day they held scented handkerchiefs to their faces to cover up the stink. Then when the rains finally came in late July, mosquitoes would breed in sewers and ditches, and the pestilence would begin.

Thus it was that every spring, long before the first case of fever was reported, King Gonzalo and his court would leave Pelenos for the country, where they would remain till late October, enjoying the cool nights, mild days, and fresh country air of the summer palace.

The building had been a seaside villa back in ancient times. And though it had been modified over the centuries, it had never strayed far from the original plan, with its long, shady porches on the eastern side, overlooking the sea, and rooms that opened onto garden courts, with their pools and trellised vines. Beyond the high walls that protected the palace, the countryside spread out to the south and west in a patchwork of orchards and fields. There, figs and olives grew, and oranges and grapes. To the north was the dense forest of the king's hunting park, well stocked with wild boar, red deer, and pheasant.

While in residence at the summer palace, the king followed a peculiar custom, begun in his grandfather's time, of living in accordance with the building and its long history. The court put away their doublets and boots, their kirtles and gowns, and dressed in togas, tunics, and sandals. They bathed every day in pools fed by natural hot springs and napped in the heat of the afternoons. In the evenings, since the villa had no great hall, they dined as the ancients had, reclining on silken couches arranged around central tables, on a large, covered porch that opened onto a garden.

The princess Elizabetta loved the summer palace.

It was everything the great, dark, opulent Lion Hall of Pelenos was not: peaceful and quiet, full of light and air. Living there was like stepping back into a simpler, more civilized age.

On this particular morning, she was sitting in her small private atrium, toying with her breakfast and watching the birds as they darted in and out of the colonnaded garden, building their nests in the beams.

Curled at her feet was an enormous cat. The slaves had named him Leondas—*lion* in the ancient tongue—because of his impressive size. He had arrived out of nowhere and attached himself to the princess, having spent his kittenhood in the vicinity of the palace kitchens—or so everyone assumed. Leondas was also watching the birds, though he was far too fat and slow to catch one. The princess gave him a fig as compensation. And the cat, who would eat anything, devoured it.

Elizabetta was feeling especially happy that morning, in a dreamy sort of way—still limp from sleep; conscious of the soft, warm air moving over her bare arms; enjoying the bright, salty taste of olives along with her bread and honey. Her senses seemed unusually sharp, as if she meant to store up every small detail of her surroundings: the intense blue of the sky overhead, the smell of rosemary from the garden, the sticky feel of honey on her fingers.

It was a moment of perfect contentment.

And then it was over.

One of her slaves came out into the atrium. She stood quietly, hands folded as was proper, waiting to be noticed.

"What is it, Giulia?" the princess asked.

The girl curtsied, then stepped closer so she wouldn't have to raise her voice.

"Your father, the king, wishes to see you, my lady. He asks you to come to his chamber."

"When?"

"Now, my lady."

"I'm not dressed."

The slave pinched her lips, unsure what to say.

"Don't be a slow-wit, Giulia. Tell me what you know. Is someone outside the door waiting for an answer?"

"No, my lady. But I think he means for you to come right away."

The princess had lately been practicing the art of mastering her own emotions. She practiced it again now, quite to her own satisfaction. She gave Giulia a nod, calmly rinsed her fingers in the bowl of lemon-water and dried them on a linen napkin, and only then did she rise to her feet.

"Well, I don't intend to go in my robe—unless there was some mention of fire or earthquake."

"There was not, my lady."

"Then I shall wear the white peplos with the lion fibulae."

"Yes, my lady. And your hair?"

"You'll braid it and bind it in the back. Something elaborate, I think."

The princess smiled, perfectly aware of how long that would take and that her father was waiting.

King Gonzalo looked up from his breakfast when his daughter came in. He'd just taken a bite of bread and was still chewing, so he waved a hand, inviting her to sit down.

"Are we at war, Father?" she asked with an innocent smile. "Such haste!"

He licked his fingers, dipped a cloth into the lemon-water, and wiped a dribble of honey from his beard. "No one is storming the gates at the moment," he said, brushing crumbs from his ample chest.

"Well, that's a relief."

The king gestured for a slave to take away the plates, then turned in his chair and settled himself—arranging his robe, pointedly taking his time. Elizabetta wiped all expression from her face and stared out the window. The sea and the morning sky were calming to look at, and she was trying very hard to hide her annoyance.

"King Reynard arrives today," he said. "I believe we can expect him before noon."

The princess had heard nothing of this visit till now. She couldn't imagine what would bring the king of Austlind to Cortova or what it had to do with her.

"You will want to look your best tonight and be especially gracious."

"Oh?" she said. "And why exactly?"

"Reynard is seeking a bride for his son, Prince Rupert. They have come to discuss the terms."

For a moment she was unable to speak. Finally, when she could manage it, "The terms?"

"The alliance. The dowry."

"I see." She managed to keep her body still, her voice under control. "But haven't you forgotten something, Father? The bride, perhaps?"

"No," he said. "I have forgotten nothing at all."

"And what if I refuse?"

"Why should you? It's your duty as princess of Cortova."

"A duty I've fulfilled twice already, if you'll recall.

You promised I'd never have to do it again."

"I only said that to stop you from screaming."

"Really, Father? Is that all your promises are worth?"

"You were unlucky; that's all. There's no reason to think such things would ever happen again. And you can't remain a maid all your life."

"*Unlucky?* Married at seven, widowed at eight? And if you think I've forgotten that time because I was so young, then you'd best think again. I've never felt so alone as I was then—in that cold, ugly palace, surrounded by a lot of strangers whose speech I couldn't understand."

"You would have adapted in time if the prince had lived. You'd have mastered the language, and made friends, and gone on to be queen of Slovarno. I believe most girls would find that a fairly tolerable life."

"Fine. We'll put that aside. It's ancient history anyway. But the match with King Edmund of Westria—"

"That was a freakish occurrence, Betta. No one could have predicted it."

"True. No one could. And yet it did happen, and I was there at his side—closer than I am to you right now—when the wolves broke into the hall and tore him apart. Do you know what it sounds like—flesh being torn? I do: it's wet. I was covered with Edmund's blood; I could smell the gore."

She took a slow, shuddering breath and glared accusingly at her father.

"That was very colorful, my dear. Are you done?" When she didn't answer, he went on. "Yes, child, I actually *do* know the sound of flesh being torn. Also the sound of sword striking bone. I know hot blood, and the stink of gore, and the reek of bowels that have been opened to the air. Some of that blood and stink was mine. I was a knight before I was king, or have you forgotten? You've seen the scars."

Her face was pale, but she didn't look away.

"It was dreadful, what happened in Westria," he said. "And I know you weren't raised to bear such things, as I was. But the hard truth is that I must have an alliance, and to get it I need the marriage."

"You never wanted an alliance before. You always said we, as a trading nation, must always remain neutral—free to buy from anyone and to sell to anyone we please."

"The situation has changed."

"Is that all you're going to tell me?"

"Yes, and more than I should have. Negotiations between kings are a subtle business, with secrets kept on both sides. Now you must keep mine."

She gave a quick little nod of assent.

"So, there it is. We are in need. You can decide to help me, or you can turn your back on your duty to Cortova and be of no use at all. Which will it be?"

He waited, giving her time to consider, observing the slow and subtle changes in the way she sat, the angle of her head and shoulders, the expression in her eyes. Then he smiled privately to himself, seeing he had won.

"Rupert is younger than you by a good four years, but he is the eldest son and will inherit. I have it on good authority that he's a sturdy and capable lad, though not especially bright."

"I've already met him, Father. Reynard was Edmund's cousin, remember? The whole family came to Westria for the wedding."

"Of course. I had forgotten."

"He struck me as sullen and proud."

The king shrugged. "Young princes often are. They grow out of it. Betta, there is something else I must tell you."

"What?"

"There's a second suitor. I've been in negotiation with both kings this past winter and spring, and have insisted that they come to me in person to discuss the terms. Now I shall play the one against the other, to our advantage."

"I am up for auction, then? Sold to the highest bid-der?"

"You could think of it that way if you wanted to be unpleasant."

"And neither of them knows—?"

"Not yet. It'll be a delicate business. I need you to be at your best."

"You haven't yet mentioned who the other suitor is. I think you're afraid to tell me. Something worse than a boy four years my junior who's sullen and none too bright. Let's see—ancient and toothless? Hideous to look upon? Somewhat too ready with his fists?"

"On the contrary, I'm told he's exceedingly hand-some, learned, and wise."

"Father—"

"It's King Alaric of Westria," he said. "Edmund's younger brother."

She held herself in check, but she leaned back and gazed up at the ceiling as she spoke.

"He's the only one who survived," she said, "of all the royal family. He'd gone to the privy, I believe, just before the wolves broke in." And then, after a pause, "He *is* handsome, Father, more so even than Edmund was. He was sweet to his mother that night, I recall. She died, too, you know. Very particular wolves they were, thirsted only for royal blood—Westrian blood."

"I'm sorry that it should be him. But it was Alaric who approached me about an alliance and a marriage, and I couldn't pass up the chance. He and Reynard may be cousins, but their kingdoms are at daggers drawn. And each hopes an alliance with us will decide the outcome. You can see the possibilities, I'm sure."

The princess studied her fingernails, thinking. "When does he arrive—Alaric?"

"Tomorrow. He was also supposed to arrive this afternoon, but there has been a delay—due to seasickness, I believe."

"They will both be here at *the same time*?"

"Yes. That's the point, Betta. Have you not been paying attention?"

She sucked in her breath, picturing the scene.

"Wear the antique diadem tonight," he said. "And perhaps a bit of powder, or whatever it is women use to make their skin look pale. Your ladies will know. We want to dazzle King Reynard."

"Do we indeed? I wonder, Father . . . What if I kept to my room instead? Or better still, wept and moaned and carried on? I'd ruin everything, wouldn't I?"

The king drummed his fingers on the arm of his chair. "Yes, daughter, you could behave like a petulant child, and embarrass yourself, and do a great deal of harm to the kingdom. But I doubt it would spoil everything. They'd probably take you kicking and screaming if it seemed to their advantage."

"But the terms—"

"—would not be nearly so advantageous."

"Exactly. So now I understand what *you* stand to gain and what Alaric and Reynard hope to achieve. What about me?"

"What *about* you?"

"My cooperation ought to be worth something, don't you think?"

"You astonish me."

"I know. I even astonish myself. So here it is, Father: if you agree to my conditions, then I will dazzle the very birds out of the trees."

"What conditions?"

"If I get you what you want from either king, on advantageous terms, then you will make me your heir."

Gonzalo threw back his head and laughed. "That's ridiculous," he said. "I already have an heir."

"I know. And what a treasure he is, too. Why, just last week your precious little Castor set a dog's tail on fire."

"He's only a child."

"No, Father, he's a little monster. And before you go on to make the obvious objections, let me point out that queens have ruled kingdoms before, and the world did not come to an end. I'm ten times cleverer than Castor at his best and nowhere near as vicious."

"I'm sorry. It's impossible. You can't expect me to disinherit my son."

"I'm sorry, too. Now I'm afraid you must excuse me. I feel a migraine coming on, and you wouldn't have me vomit on your carpet."

She rose, curtsied to her father, then walked slowly and gracefully toward the door. A slave stepped forward to open it. Elizabetta sailed right through. She was already out in the hall when she heard her father's voice.

"Wait," he said.

❧ 2 ❧

Like Shepherds

REYNARD AND HIS PARTY of knights and retainers arrived shortly before noon. They were met at the entry gate by King Gonzalo's steward, who summoned grooms to see to their horses and slaves to unload their trunks. Then he led the party out of the stable yard, through the palace gate, and into a large entry garden.

"If your men will kindly wait here, Your Grace, they will be offered refreshments. I will escort you and Prince Rupert to my lord King Gonzalo. He's aware that you've been traveling and are probably tired, but he did want to welcome you in person. I assure you it won't take long."

"Of course. We would be honored."

"Very well then—this way. His Majesty is in the council chamber."

They found Gonzalo dressed in an everyday toga and sandals, dictating letters to a scribe. Reynard bowed, exactly calculating the degree of deference one ruler owes to another. But the king of Cortova ignored protocol altogether, leaping up from his chair and, smiling broadly, welcoming them with outstretched arms.

"Reynard!" he boomed, as boisterous as a child. "How many years has it been? I do believe I had just begun to shave when last we met. Where was it now— at the marriage of my uncle Lorenzo to your wife's cousin, Constantia?"

"My lady's aunt, actually."

"Of course, of course—the aunt! Oh, but that *does* make me feel old. So many years! And this handsome lad must be young Prince Rupert, already grown and as tall as you are! Where *have* the years gone?"

Reynard had heard tales about King Gonzalo, but they hadn't prepared him for this. Everything was odd: his strange behavior, his casual dress, and the informal way that everything was said and done. Reynard couldn't quite decide whether the man was demented or was playing some subtle game. Well, if it was the latter and his goal was to put Reynard off balance, then he'd certainly succeeded.

"I know you must be travel-weary, so I won't keep you any longer. My steward will take you to your quarters. You can relax a bit, have something to eat, and wash away the dust of the road. The slaves will bring your belongings, of course, and help you get settled."

Reynard bowed again but only half as low this time. "Thank you for your thoughtfulness," he said.

"As for this evening . . . well, I must explain that the summer palace has no great hall. It wasn't the custom back in the days when this great old heap of an antique ruin was built. So we usually dine in accordance with the ancient traditions of the house."

Reynard had heard tales about this, too: how Gonzalo and his guests sprawled out on silken couches, dressed in togas like the emperors of yore. But Reynard had not believed them. Those had struck him as the sort of colorful details people feel compelled to add when they can't resist making a good story better.

"But alas, our dining space, while extremely charming, is also very small—only room for nine, you know, which won't do for a royal banquet. So I apologize in advance for the informality, but we're setting things up on the landing out back, overlooking the garden. Terribly rustic, I'm afraid," he said.

"Like shepherds," he added with a smile.

Demented, Reynard decided as he left. *No question about it.*

⚜

On the way to the guest quarters, the steward filled them in on the protocol—or lack thereof—for that evening's banquet. There would be no grand entrances according to rank, as was the common custom. They'd be dining outside, after all, so such formalities would seem contrived and artificial. And King Gonzalo preferred to get there first so he could greet his guests as they arrived.

Reynard didn't like this at all. He was a firm believer in established tradition. It honored the great as was fitting, formalized courtesy and made things run smoothly, and spelled out exactly what was expected so everyone knew his place and what he was supposed to do. For a king to go first into his own banquet and welcome his guests—as though he were the bloody *porter* or something—well, it was downright offensive.

But Reynard kept his irritation in check. He needed this alliance, however mad the king might be, not only for the obvious advantages it would bring, but to prevent his cousin Alaric from getting it himself.

The balance between their two kingdoms, Austlind

and Westria, had been tilting in Reynard's favor for some time. Alaric lacked the support of his noblemen, who thought him too young and inexperienced to rule. There'd been plots and counterplots, with pretty much everyone agreeing that the boy needed a regent to run the kingdom for him but with no one agreeing as to who that person should be. Reynard had hoped—no, fully expected—that a nice little civil war would soon break out, opening the door for him to step in and solve everything.

But then, in early autumn, the balance had begun to tilt in the other direction. Lord Mayhew—heretofore Alaric's bitterest enemy and the chief conspirator—had inexplicably gone over to the king, urging the rest of the nobles to follow his example. By winter all the feathers had been smoothed, control had been reestablished, and Mayhew was busy building the king's forces into a formidable and disciplined army.

It was true that Alaric had never shown any inclination to attack Reynard—but then he hadn't had much of an army before. Now he did; and if he aligned his kingdom with Cortova (as was rumored he might), and married the princess, and got himself an heir—well, that would be the end of it for Austlind.

That's why, these past eight months, Reynard had been courting the reluctant king of Cortova. He'd even agreed to come and negotiate in person—an outrageous demand on Gonzalo's part—and had resigned himself to paying a king's ransom if he must and making whatever concessions might be required, just so long as he got that alliance and Alaric did not.

Now, apparently, he would also have to go to this farce of a banquet—where they'd eat like bloody shepherds in a bloody meadow—and do his very best to be gracious, maybe even obsequious if it was absolutely called for. He just bloody well hoped they wouldn't have to eat on the ground.

As it turned out, they would not.

 ⤐ ⤏

Shortly after sunset, a small group of slaves, all dressed in the black-and-gold livery of Cortova and all of them carrying lanterns, appeared at the door of Reynard's guesthouse. They had come to escort the party from Austlind to the king of Cortova's humble banquet.

After a rather lengthy walk—through the north gate, down a series of long colonnades, turning left, then right, then left again—they finally came out onto a wide stone landing overlooking an expansive garden. There, trestle tables sufficient for any banquet in any great hall had been set up in the conventional U-shaped pattern, with a high table in the center and a long row of tables extending on either side. All the tables were draped in sea-blue damask, just pale enough to reflect the light of at least five hundred candles but dark enough to set off the countless arrangements of white roses, one set between each of the many candlestands. A silver platter rested at every place, along with a silver-gilt goblet, a silver spoon, and one of those newfangled forks that were all the rage these days.

Overhead, in the clear evening sky, the stars were just coming out. Below, in the garden, hundreds of little lanterns hung from the trees. And in the dark places beyond the lanterns' reach, fireflies danced like fairies in the night. Soft music filled the air around them, seeming as much a part of the natural world as the sighing of the wind in the branches and the distant crashing of waves on the shore.

As Reynard and his party arrived, slaves stepped forward to offer them wine: chilled in ice that had been carried down from the mountains, served in cups of frosted green glass, clearly more than a thousand years old. Reynard had treasures of his own back in Austlind, but nothing compared to this! And how many of those cups were there, anyway? There had to be a hundred at least. Why, some ancient emperor might have drunk from the very cup Reynard now held to his lips. Truly, it took his breath away.

Obviously he would have to rethink Gonzalo. For those antique cups were more than just the usual display of wealth and taste. They'd been brought out to send a subtle but unmistakable message: that when those glasses were made, Gonzalo's forebears were masters of the known world, builders of great cities, aqueducts, and bridges—while Reynard's ancestors were little more than savages living in wattle huts, wearing animal skins, and smearing their bodies with blue woad and grease before going, half naked, into battle.

God's bones, Reynard thought; he'd have to keep his wits about him!

And now here came Gonzalo himself, smiling warmly, dressed in a toga of the finest wool, soft as silk, trimmed with delicate embroidery. And in harmony with his theme of ancient grandeur, his crown was a laurel wreath of beaten gold studded with pearls.

"Welcome to my hall," he said, all hint of buffoonery gone. "I hope you are well rested and have come with a healthy appetite. I have planned a very special dinner in your honor."

And suddenly it all seemed terribly funny to Reynard: the comical way Gonzalo had played him for a fool and how easily he'd fallen for the joke, and now this astonishing dinner out under the stars with people dressed in ancient costumes and invisible musicians playing from somewhere, probably behind a boxwood hedge. And with the hilarity came a rush of warmth and high spirits.

Reynard clapped his host on the shoulder with a manly hand, then leaned back his head and roared with laughter.

"Like shepherds!" he said, and laughed again.

{ 3 }

The Princess
and Her Mirror

THE PRINCESS LOOKED INTO her mirror. A face of astonishing beauty gazed back. But Elizabetta didn't smile at her own reflection. She already knew the effects of the many expressions she had at her command and when to bring them out to best advantage, just as a swordsman knows the variations on attack, parry, and riposte and how they can be used most effectively in combat.

And that's exactly how she thought of her beauty: as a weapon, nothing more. She certainly hadn't earned it, any more than she'd arranged to be born the daughter of a king. But while she took no credit for her great good fortune, she was perfectly aware of the power it gave her to achieve her goals—so long as she didn't fall into the trap of self-admiration. That would be like turning her own weapon on herself.

This was rare wisdom indeed. She'd learned it from her mother long ago.

The princess had been only six when the queen, near death from childbed fever, had summoned her daughter to the royal bedchamber one last time. Betta remembered how dark and close the chamber had been that day—though it was late afternoon, the shutters had been drawn over all the windows, and the room was dimly lit by candles.

"I'm dying, sweet child," the queen had said, reaching out to take Betta's hand. "I'm so very sorry. But before I go, I have a special gift for you."

Elizabetta's eyes had darted nervously around the room, wondering which of her mother's many treasures it might be.

"It's not that kind of gift, dearest," the queen had said. "This is something far more precious—hard-won knowledge that will prepare you for the years that lie ahead. I meant to wait till you were older and more capable of understanding, but it seems I cannot. So you must listen carefully and remember what I say. Will you do that?"

"Yes," Elizabetta had said in a small, small voice, wringing her hands and trying not to cry.

"I know that you'll be sad when I'm gone. There are already tears in your eyes, just at the thought of losing me. Is that because I'm beautiful and you won't get to look at my face anymore?"

The princess had blinked in confusion.

"Is that the reason?"

"I don't want you to go away," she'd said, sobbing now, "because you're my mother, and I love you."

"Because I'm beautiful?"

"No."

"Because I'm the great queen of Cortova?"

"No."

"Thank you, child. Those were the right answers. You love me because you know I love you. Because I hold you in my arms and make you feel safe. Because I tell you stories, and kiss your head, and make you laugh. Because I listen to you when you have something to say and treat you with respect, even though you're just a little child."

The princess nodded. That was exactly why she loved her mother.

"Good. You understand what love is. Hold on to

that; you're going to need it.

"Throughout your life, people will admire you and praise you. They'll seek you out because your father is the king, and they'll gasp with pleasure when you enter a room because you're such a beauty. But don't for a minute think that means they love you—or even like you, for that matter. They might, or they might not, once they get to know you, once they've seen how you behave in different situations and are able to judge whether you're clever and kind or shallow, selfish, and vain. But few will bother to notice those things.

"Betta, the hard truth is that those people aren't interested in you at all—only in what you can do for them. They'll bask in the reflected glory of being the princess's friend, they'll hope you will further their advancement, and they'll enjoy the many delights of life at court. But if you were reduced to poverty and lost your looks, they wouldn't give you a second glance."

The princess had been confused by these words. Was her mother angry? Had she done something wrong?

"I know all this because I was a princess, too. And when I was young, I was almost as lovely as you. I thought very highly of myself and spent a shocking amount of time gazing into mirrors, smiling and posing."

She made a cloying face to demonstrate. But she was weak from the fever, so the effect was more grotesque than she'd intended.

"I loved being petted and praised. I thought I deserved it, you see. I thought it was real. Then one day I overheard a conversation between two of the court ladies. They were talking about me. They laughed and called me ridiculous. I blush to think how shocked I was. Truly, I had no idea. I honestly believed that everyone admired me . . . because I was a princess and because I was pretty.

"So this is my gift to you, dearest Betta, wisdom I paid for with my tears: If you want to be truly loved, then you must be worthy of love. If you want to be fairly praised, accomplish something."

Betta had cried herself to sleep that night, and early the next morning she'd been told her mother was dead. Weeks later, after the queen had been laid to rest with all due ceremony, the king had given his daughter a pretty little fruitwood box inlaid with ivory and gold—a gift from her mother, he'd said; the queen had particularly wanted Betta to have it.

Later, in her room, the princess had opened the box and found the real gift inside: her mother's dying words all written out, so Betta would never forget a single thing.

She'd read that letter many times since then. And as each year passed, she'd understood it better, picking up subtleties that had been beyond a child of six, or ten, or thirteen. Now, as she faced the greatest challenge of her life, Elizabetta armed herself with her mother's wisdom, planned her attack, chose her weapons, and honed them to a glistening edge.

She'd lived her whole life at court—not only in Cortova, but also in Slovarno, where she'd been crown princess for a year and five months, and later for a very short time in Westria. And so she'd seen every possible form of feminine adornment—from silks, lace, velvets, furs, feathers, veils, and jewels to steeple caps, false hair, kohl-lined eyes, plucked brows, rouged cheeks, and whitened skin. Reynard and his son would have seen them, too, a thousand times and more.

She would give them something altogether different.

✦ ✦

"But my lady, are you *sure* you wouldn't rather wear the gold chiton with the lavender palla?"

"Because—?"

"It's so very grand and beautiful."

"And with a chiton I must wear eight fibulae, not just two. So much shinier—all that gold."

"It *is* a special occasion, my lady."

"Estella, when you become a princess and have a royal banquet to attend, you may wear my gold chiton. Until that time, please bring me the saffron peplos. I'll line it with cream and wrap it with pale blue—the palla *without* the fringe, please."

"Of course, my lady. I'm sure you're right. Why cover your beautiful arms with a great, bulky chiton?"

"Why indeed?"

Simple though the peplos was, the princess had given careful thought to her choice. She was aware, for example, that the saffron silk was exceptionally fine; it would catch the candlelight and glow like cloth-of-gold. And the pale blue mantle, when draped across her chest and over her shoulder, would draw the eye up to her face.

Now she sat before her mirror, not smiling, while Giulia began to oil and brush her hair as she always did.

"What do you think?" the slave asked. "Shall we build it very high to set off the diadem? Side coils would show it off nicely as well, but they're so common now."

"No. Just draw it back into a single braid, rather loose, if you will."

"But that's for every day, my lady, not for suitors!"

"Nevertheless . . ."

Giulia thought her mistress must surely have gone mad. But she did as she was told, smoothing back the princess's long, thick hair, then dividing it into three equal sections and deftly weaving the strands into a heavy braid. When she had finished, she fastened the end with a white silk ribbon to which she pinned a small golden ornament: a lion with tiny emerald eyes. Perhaps the princess didn't notice. At any rate, she didn't object.

"Now," said Estella, kneeling beside the princess with the jewelry coffer open in her hands. "Which necklace will you wear, my lady?"

Giulia shot her a warning look, which Estella failed to notice. "May I suggest—?"

"No, Estella, you may not. I'll wear the small pearl earrings and the diadem. Nothing else."

"*No necklace?*"

"What did I just say?"

"But *why*, my lady? Merchants' wives in Pelenos wear ten times more jewelry than that!"

Claudia, the elderly freedwoman who ran the princess's household and had charge of all the slaves, had been listening to this in silence from her special chair. Now she removed Leondas, who'd been purring contentedly in her lap, rose ponderously to her feet, and drew the young slave aside.

"My dear," she said gently, "I can see that you mean well, but the princess knows exactly what she wants."

"Yes, but—"

"Tell me, Estella—when you saw those merchants' wives in Pelenos, what did you really see?"

"I'm sorry; I don't understand."

"What do you recall? Could you describe one of them to me right now?"

"I . . . well, there was this particular necklace; it had three gold chains of varying lengths so that the top one held the whole thing together; then the next one hung below it, you see, making a nice little curve, like this; and then the longest one—"

"I can imagine it. What else?"

"Well, it all came together in the middle, where there was this very large ruby drop with pearls all around it."

"You were very observant, Estella. Now describe the lady who wore it."

The girl blinked, embarrassed.

"Old or young?"

"Not young. But not what you'd call old."

"Dark or fair?"

"I *think* her hair was dark."

"But you're not sure."

"No."

"Estella, there are two reasons a woman wears elaborate gowns and lots of jewels. One is to display her wealth. The other is to make her look more attractive."

She paused to let the slave take this in.

"Do you think my lady needs to remind her suitor that her father is rich?"

"Of course not. Everyone knows that he is a king!"

"And would you say that her appearance needs improving?"

"Not at all!"

"Exactly. Now our lady princess is going to meet one of her suitors tonight. When he returns to his quarters after the dinner and thinks back on the evening, what would she like him to remember?"

"That she is beautiful."

"Not how the chains on her necklace draped so cunningly or the size of the ruby that hung down in the middle?"

"No, Claudia."

"Good. I believe we understand each other. Now go help my lady with her earrings."

"Yes, Claudia."

With trembling hands, Estella took the pearl drops from the coffer and threaded the gold loops through the little holes in the princess's earlobes. Then she stepped away, and Giulia came forward with the case that held the diadem.

This crown, like the summer palace itself, was ancient, a relic of Cortova's grandest age. It was delicate and finely made, its gold burnished to a soft sheen by the touch of countless regal hands over the course of a thousand years. Elizabetta now took it reverently and set it upon her own head, deeply conscious of the history it carried and of all the long-dead queens and princesses who'd worn it before. Over the ages their lives had been reduced to a few dry footnotes in history books, yet they'd each witnessed some small part of the great arc of Cortova's history. They'd been consorts to kings of famous name or miserable child brides who'd died very young. They'd seen conquest and glory, treachery and murder, famine, war, and plague. But each of them, whatever her story might have been, had probably sat before a mirror, just as she did now, looking at her reflection, admiring the beautiful diadem, and thinking of the evening ahead.

And like them—just this once—Elizabetta smiled.

≹ 4 ≹

The First Suitor

SLAVES MOVED THROUGH THE crowd with silver trays, collecting the antique cups. Others followed with laurel wreaths for the gentlemen to wear. They weren't gold like Gonzalo's, but they were handsomely made: the leaves fresh and fragrant, the wreaths fastened in the back with silk ribbons. But for Reynard and his son, as guests of honor (who were already wearing crowns), Gonzalo had provided something special and distinctive: long strips of cloth-of-gold to be worn across the chest and fastened at the shoulder with a golden pin (also, apparently, a gift).

While the slaves who'd brought the sashes were

making a few fine adjustments—the pin must lie a little to the front so it would show to advantage, and the loose ends of the fabric must be smoothed down so as to hang properly—Reynard looked around and noticed for the first time that there were no ladies in attendance.

Not a single one.

Not even the princess.

Did Gonzalo really expect him to agree to a match with his son—and pay handsomely for the privilege—without even so much as laying eyes on the girl?

Well, of course, now that he thought of it, he *had* laid eyes on her that night in Westria. She'd come floating into the banquet hall of Dethemere Castle on the arm of King Edmund the Fair, and no one in the room had looked at anyone but her. The hall had buzzed with a chorus of whispers and sighs, all of them remarking on her beauty: those large, dark eyes; that creamy skin; the dramatic nose; and the hair as sleek and black as a raven's wing. She'd worn a head-dress, he remembered, of gold netting encrusted with emeralds and pearls. The pearls had glistened against her dark hair like stars in a winter sky.

So, considering that she was such a paragon of loveliness, why not bring her out and show her off? He supposed it didn't really matter whether Rupert wed a gnome or a goddess so long as Reynard got his alliance and the girl could produce an heir. But still, it was strange.

Slaves now began directing the guests to their seats. Reynard, as the principal guest of honor, was at King Gonzalo's right hand. Rupert was two seats down from his father, an empty place between them.

At last everyone was settled. Now they all waited, as custom demanded, for their host to sit down. But this he seemed strangely reluctant to do. So they stood in silence for an uncommonly long time.

The delay clearly had something to do with the missing guests. There must be fifteen or twenty of them, judging by the empty places at the tables, including one to the king's left and the one between Reynard and his son. Either Gonzalo's courtiers were incredibly rude—it was unthinkable to arrive late for a royal banquet!—or the Cortovans had some peculiar social custom having to do with the absent women. Most likely the latter, Reynard decided. Everything was peculiar in Cortova.

Just as he was thinking this, the ethereal music, which had been playing softly in the background, grew bolder and more festive as a procession emerged from the trees in the garden below.

It was led by two files of young female slaves all

dressed in white and carrying lamps. With remarkable precision, they spaced themselves out along the path ahead till they'd formed a wall of light for those who followed.

The princess now appeared, walking hand in hand with her little brother, Prince Castor. The royal children were followed by the ladies of the court, walking in pairs, their colorful tunics ruffling in the breeze. As the procession neared the wide staircase that led up to the landing, the wall of light moved with them till they'd reached the top. There the two rows of slaves parted and moved to the sides like a shimmering bird spreading its wings.

The prince and princess came forward and made obeisance to their father—he with a manly bow, she with a graceful curtsy—then went around the table and took their places. The ladies of the court followed suit, two at a time. Only when the last of them was standing at her place did King Gonzalo finally sit down.

⚜

In preparation for this visit, Prince Rupert had been given lessons in the language of Cortova by a tiresome old scold of a schoolmaster. But he hadn't paid a bit of attention. Later, during the journey south, Rupert's nonexistent skills had been "polished" by one of his father's knights who'd lived for some time on the borderlands and prided himself on his flawless Cortovan accent. The prince had learned nothing from him, either.

And really, what was the point? Rupert wasn't the one who had to negotiate with King Gonzalo. He was just along for show—to assure Cortova that he was neither an idiot nor a leper, which was surely all they really cared about. And besides, after he and the princess were married, she'd have to learn *his* language. So why bother? Wasn't he doing enough as it was just going on this tiresome journey and sitting through another one of those boring, everlasting, stupid banquets?

He'd been relieved, when they'd been shown to their seats, that the place to his left was empty. That meant he'd only have to deal with one person: the aged crone on his right, the duchess Somebody-or-other. Since she was most likely deaf and senile, she wouldn't notice what he said no matter what language he said it in. And if he got really bored, he could always talk across the empty seat to his father. Not that he liked his father all that much.

When the ladies' procession had first appeared in the garden, Rupert had taken it for the entertainment.

He'd wondered why they were starting so early, before the guests had even taken their seats. But he'd figured it out when the boy went to stand beside Gonzalo and the girl took the empty place next to him.

For the past six months Rupert's friends had been telling him how beautiful the princess was supposed to be and saying how lucky he was. Rupert had always replied that he knew *all* about it. He'd seen her in Westria—and she wasn't bad at all.

But the truth was, he honestly didn't remember her from that night. He'd been younger then and in a mood because he hadn't wanted to go to Westria for the stupid wedding of some stupid relative he'd never even met. He'd been too busy making steeples with his fingers and kicking his brothers under the table to notice one girl out of a hundred who'd paraded into the hall.

But now that he was going to marry her and she was apparently such a beauty—well, naturally he was curious. So once they were seated, he turned to have a look.

Even Rupert knew it would be rude just to stare. He had to say something. So he brought out what he thought he remembered meant *hello* in Cortovan—though apparently it didn't, because she seemed a bit confused. She said something back to him, which of course he didn't understand, so he just nodded.

Yes, he decided, she was definitely pretty, no question about it—though as a general rule he preferred girls with fair hair and pert little turned-up noses. But her skin was exceptional—perhaps a little dark, but then the Cortovans *were* a swarthy people—and her lips were just about as good as they come.

But what struck him speechless was the fact that she hadn't even bothered to dress up or do fancy things with her hair. And where were the jewels? Surely she had some; the king of Cortova was famously rich. Yet aside from the little pearl earrings she wore and that gold thing on her head (which was too small to be a proper crown and was old and worn besides), there wasn't so much as a bracelet or a ring, much less a necklace.

The princess was smiling now, and that in itself was something to behold: those teeth—God's breath, they were perfect! But now she was speaking again, saying something else Rupert couldn't make head nor tail of. Finally he gave it up for hopeless and attended to his wine.

The princess, however, was not so easily discouraged. She tried again, this time in Westrian. She didn't speak it well, but she'd studied it for a time in preparation for her marriage to Edmund. She apparently guessed that if Prince Rupert knew any other language at all, it would likely be Westrian, since the two kingdoms shared a border and were linked by family ties. Her guess proved to be correct.

"You like the fig?" she asked sweetly as the first course was served.

"Yes," he grunted, thinking how long and slender her neck was: swanlike—that's how the court singers usually described such a feature in their ballads of the heroes and ladies.

"It grow here in garden with sun. Is also oranges we have. And grapes for wine."

"Mmm," he said.

"Too hot you like, in the day?"

He shrugged.

Reynard had been watching them. Now he leaned forward and shot his son a look that would have peeled the hide off a boar. The prince recoiled and attempted a smile, which was so transparently false as to be grotesque.

The king of Austlind shut his eyes and sighed.

~❧ ❦~

When the servers had retreated and the feast was well under way, Gonzalo made a signal and the entertainment began.

It started with drums, slow and deep. *Boom! Boom! Boom! Boom! Boom! Boom!* Soon they were joined by the rhythmic jangle of tambourines. Finally, over the pulsing percussion, flutes and krummhorns began to play, exotic and wild, as a troupe of dancers from Aegyptos came leaping out of the darkness into the space embraced by the three long tables and stood at attention like soldiers.

They were dressed in loincloths of a fiery red, a rainbow of bright-colored ribbons hanging from the waistbands, at the end of which were little brass bells. But apart from their loincloths—and the gold armbands and wide gold collars they wore, which shone like fire against their dark skin glistening with oil— they were entirely naked.

Now the dance began with a rhythmic slapping of bare feet on stone—thrilling in its complex cadence— growing louder and faster until the tension was almost unbearable. Then they broke away from their martial formation and began a battle dance. It was intricate, and ferocious, and beautiful all at once. The audience forgot the feast and held their breaths as they watched.

✢ ✢

Reynard took this opportunity to study the princess (looking at her sideways so as not to be too obvious, though she seemed too absorbed by the dancers to notice) and was puzzled, as his son had been, by her lack of adornment. Had she mislaid her net with the emeralds and pearls? Taken a vow of simplicity? Overslept so she hadn't had time to do herself up properly?

The princess felt his gaze just then and turned and smiled.

Reynard had heard stories of great magicians who could slay dragons with a flick of their willow wands and of the basilisk that could kill with a single glance. Elizabetta's smile had been almost as powerful. And for a moment the king of Austlind felt his chest grow tight so that he could hardly breathe.

"Are you quite well, Your Grace?" she asked.

"I am, yes, my lady."

"You looked a little wan. But then, you've traveled such a long way. You must be quite exhausted."

"I am, a little."

Oh, you fool, he thought. *How can you be a little exhausted? A little tired, maybe, but—*

She laid a hand gently on Reynard's arm, just above the wrist. He jumped at her touch, but she was gracious enough not to notice. She just leaned in with a conspiratorial grin. "I shouldn't tell, but there are some remarkable fancies yet to come, and one of them was made especially for you."

He felt very much like a boy of seven being promised a packet of lavender drops if he was very, very good.

"And at the risk of spoiling the surprise, well, I'll just say that it's quite enormous and made entirely of egg whites, honey, and heaven knows what else, and that when you see it you will recognize it. There! Something to look forward to, no matter how tired you are."

Reynard was not quite taking this in. He was noticing the fine arch of her brow, the angle of her cheekbones, the soft curve of her lips, and that amazing, delicate complexion—untouched by paint or powder—which positively glowed with the freshness of youth.

And he sensed, without quite understanding it, that he saw her perfection now, as he hadn't before, precisely *because* she was so simply arrayed. He wasn't distracted by other things—such as pearls and emeralds sparkling in her hair. And it came to him that this was exactly how she'd planned it.

Could she really be as clever as that? If so, then heaven help his son!

The music was reaching its crescendo now, the dancers spinning in unison, their arms upraised, the colored ribbons flying out around them like the petals of a flower.

"Yee-yee-yee-yee-yee-yee-yee-*YEE!*" they cried, their high-pitched voices supported by the rapid beating of the drums—louder and louder, faster and faster. And then *BOOM!*—one final clap of thunder, and in an instant it was over. The dancers remained frozen, arms still stretched toward the heavens. And for just the time it takes to draw a breath, everything was still.

Then the silence was broken by a roar of laughter and applause, and the princess removed her hand from Reynard's arm.

"Also," she whispered, "right after the sweets, there will be fireworks."

Well, of course, he thought. *Fireworks. Why not?*

Several Days Before

❦ 5 ❧

Premonitions

THE KING OF WESTRIA knocked on the door to Molly's cabin and was admitted by her attendant.

"Your Grace!" said the lady, blushing and dropping into a very deep curtsy.

"Leave us" was all he said, and she did.

The king crossed the room—it only took two steps—and stood over the little cot, examining the disheveled heap of bedclothes. He touched the blanket and encountered a shoulder.

"Molly?" he said.

She grunted softly.

"You are aware, I believe, that protocol requires

you to rise in the presence of your king." When she answered this with a derisive snort, he grinned. "You could at least sit up so I can see your face."

"Not worth looking at," she mumbled. "And besides, I'm not sure I can."

"Then I shall help you."

He threw back the blanket and took her in his arms, lifting and settling her in a seated position as easily as if she'd been a child. He tucked a pillow behind her back, then drew up the covers again.

"You *are* a mess," he agreed, brushing tangles of damp hair from her face.

"Just the dried husk of my former self," she said drowsily, "hollow and crumbling to dust. Soon the wind will come and blow me away."

The ship lurched. She shut her eyes and furrowed her brow. "How is it that even though I'm emptied out entire, I still feel like I'm going to puke?"

"It'll be over soon. We're due to reach port tomorrow."

She swallowed the bile that had risen in her throat and shuddered.

"Have you been drinking the restorative I sent? You must have fluids, Molly, whether you eat or not."

"I had some of it this morning. Tobias all but forced it down my throat."

"Good for Tobias. I shall do the same. Where is it?"

She responded with a feeble wave in the general direction of her knees.

"What, under the *bedclothes*?"

"It's in there somewhere, I think."

"Oh, for heaven's sake!"

He pulled back the covers again and searched—muttering to himself about the indignity of it all, and how in blazes had it come to this?—till at last he found the bottle wedged between the bulkhead and the mattress.

He rescued it and removed the cork. Then, taking Molly's chin in one hand and the bottle in the other, he tipped a little liquid onto her tongue.

"Just sip it; that's right. If you take it a bit at a time, you're more likely to keep it down. And just so you know, you're going to finish this bottle before I leave. Then I will send you another. You'll drink that one, too. Understand?"

"Alaric, I really need—"

"I know. Tobias told me." He dragged a chair from the corner and sat down beside the cot. "One more sip, and I'll hear you out."

She drank it, fought off another a wave of nausea, then took a deep breath and looked squarely at the king.

"Alaric," she said, so softly that he had to lean forward to hear, "you know how, before a storm, the clouds build and grow dark, and the wind picks up and feels suddenly cooler—it even has a different smell? You can feel in your bones that it's going to rain, and rain hard. Well, sometimes it's like that for me. I get a powerful foreboding of things to come. It looms over me like a storm cloud. That's how it's been these last days, ever since we set sail."

He nodded, all attention.

"Last night I had a vision—I've learned to tell the difference now between commonplace dreams and visions that come to me in my sleep."

"And this was a vision."

"Yes, a very strange one. I was in a garden—like in the abbey, remember? With covered walkways on all four sides? Only this was small. There was a pool in the middle, and there were lots of flowers. I was alone except for a very big yellow cat, and he was speaking to me."

"The cat?"

"Yes. He said, 'In chess, the object of the game is to protect your king.'"

"Molly, that's nonsense."

"Wait. I'm not finished. I said, 'I'm not playing chess—I don't even know how—so why are you telling me that?' And the cat started pacing back and forth, but he didn't answer. So I asked the question differently, because I thought I already knew the answer. I said, 'Are you warning me that my king is in danger?' And he said, 'Yes.' Then I asked him what kind of danger, and he admitted he didn't know, not yet at least. It could be that the danger was still forming. But he'd hoped I might be able to figure it out. And if not, well, at least I could warn you to stay on your guard."

"That's it?"

"No. There's more. I felt—in this vision—as if I were about to leave, but the cat was calling me back. He said, 'Didn't you wonder why King Gonzalo insisted that your king come in person to discuss the terms of the marriage and the alliance? Is that the way such matters are usually arranged?' And I said that as far as I knew—which wasn't very far at all—it was more common to work things out through messengers. But as it happened, going to Cortova was convenient for my king. By which, of course, I meant that you have to give the Loving Cup to the princess in person in order for the enchantment to work. But I didn't tell the cat that part, because I wasn't sure I could trust him."

"Molly, I'm trying very hard to take this seriously, but do you have any idea how comical it sounds?"

"Of course I do. But I'll let you judge when I've told you everything."

"All right."

"So the cat said, 'Think, Molly. Gonzalo neither knows nor cares that it's convenient for your king. In fact, he believes just the opposite, that's it's a long journey at an awkward and dangerous time for him to be away, considering how things are between Westria and Austlind. So oughtn't you ask yourself why?'"

She'd been speaking with her eyes closed; it helped her concentrate. But now she opened them and looked directly at Alaric. She could see that he was considering what she'd just said, and that it had alarmed him.

"So the cat asked, 'Are you aware that King Reynard of Austlind *also* seeks an alliance with Cortova and hopes to marry his eldest son to the princess?' 'Yes,' I said. 'We've heard that rumor. But if they'd already come to terms, Gonzalo wouldn't have summoned Alaric, so that obviously means—' But the cat didn't even let me finish. He said, *'Really?'* and gave me this knowing look. 'Are you *sure*?' And that's when I started to put it all together."

"Molly, are you—was the cat—suggesting that Cortova and Austlind have already formed an alliance; and as part of their arrangement, Gonzalo has lured

me away from home so Reynard can attack my kingdom?"

"That was my first thought, yes. But then—"

"What?"

"I reminded myself that Lord Mayhew remains in
Westria, and you'd defer to him in military matters
anyway since your skills don't lie in that direction. So
your absence would be *regrettable*—"

"But of no real importance. I understand."

"Alaric, forgive me, but Reynard doesn't *need* to
attack us. You're the last living member of the royal
house of Westria, and you have no heir. As your first
cousin, Reynard is quite legitimately the next in line
for the throne. It would be so much easier, and less
costly—and certainly it would *look* much better to the
world at large—if he just . . . I mean, if he and the king
of Cortova really are in collusion, and you've been
drawn away from the safety of your castle . . . Do you
think he might . . . ?"

"Arrange an accident?"

"Something like that. More or less."

Wordlessly, the king uncorked the bottle and
gave her another sip. On impulse, she grabbed it and
drank down the elixir—*glug, glug, glug*—then shivered,
burped, and dropped the bottle onto the coverlet.

"Goodness!" said the king, impressed.

"Double your guard, Alaric. And don't trust any-one in the court of Cortova."

The king leaned back and gazed thoughtfully out the tiny porthole, where a brisk wind was flinging sea spray up against the glass.

"How could I possibly have missed it?" he said, shaking his head in wonder. "It's so obvious now that you've said it."

"You missed it—we both did—because it fell in with our plans."

"I suppose you're right."

He got to his feet and dragged the chair back over to the corner. There he stood for a moment, thinking his private thoughts. Molly had shut her eyes again. The talking had worn her out.

"Once we land," he said, "we'll stay on at the inn for as long as you need to recover. After that it's an easy three-day ride to the summer palace."

"Mmm," she said, already drifting back to sleep.

He continued to stand there, his hand resting on the back of the chair, searching for the words that ought to be said: how deeply indebted he was to her; how much he relied upon her wisdom, her courage, and the magical gift that led her.

And then—oh, for heaven's sake! *Relied upon? Indebted?* Those were words he might use when speaking to Mayhew or Lord Brochton. They didn't even begin to express what he owed to Molly, or what he felt, or what he feared, or the terrible sadness that crept over him as they moved inexorably toward the thing he would have to do—because he was king now, and the welfare of Westria must be his paramount concern.

From the bed he heard a soft little snore. Molly had slipped from her upright position and was tilted toward the bulkhead, her head resting against the wall, her hair in her face, and her mouth open. For some reason, seeing her like that made Alaric want to weep.

So he just said, "Thank you," very softly, and left it at that.

⟪ 6 ⟫

The Gift

AS THEY NEARED THE coast of Cortova, the seas grew calmer and the ship sailed more smoothly than before. Molly was up now, having herself dressed by Esther, her lady attendant. They were due to disembark in a matter of hours.

She was terribly weak, having eaten nothing for days. But Molly had her pride (and an important role to play), so she fervently hoped that Esther could transform her once again into the lady Marguerite of Barcliffe Manor, because at the moment she far more resembled her old, original self: Molly, the tailor's daughter from nowhere.

Esther had plenty with which to work, so it shouldn't have been a problem. Molly was pretty to begin with, blessed as she was with fine eyes and remarkably luminous skin. And she certainly had everything a lady might need in the way of gowns and jewels. But she'd lost weight this past week, and her gowns didn't fit anymore. Her once-beautiful complexion had turned sallow, almost gray. And the less said about her hair the better.

The transformation was going to be a challenge.

"Any chance you could take the gown up a little?" Molly asked.

"Yes, of course, my lady, if we had enough time."

"But we don't."

"No, my lady."

"Then we'll have to make do by tightening the laces. How about my hair? Can you work any wonders?"

"Well, my lady, it *is* a bit, um—"

"Disheveled? Unkempt?"

"Oh, no, my lady. It's just that you've been lying abed these many days—"

"Tossing and sweating. I understand. It's oily, and matted, and pressed into strange formations no longer resembling curls."

"Well, naturally it *would* be better if we could wash

it. But there wouldn't be near enough time for it to dry."

"Can you draw it up into a knot in back and make a fringe of curls on the sides? I liked it when you did that before."

"I could, my lady, though it might be dangerous— the curling iron so close to your face on a rocking ship."

"Then what are we to do? I can't go out like this."

"No, my lady. It seems there are only two possibilities. One, we could braid the hair tight against your head. It won't be elegant, but you'll look nice and tidy, and you could always add a spray of pearls or something."

"And the other possibility?"

"Risk the curling and use a towel to protect your cheeks."

"Well," Molly said, "I've always preferred to be risky than tidy. Set the iron in the lamp and find me a cloth, and we'll just hope for the best."

When the curling had been accomplished with no mishaps whatsoever, Molly looked into her mirror and was satisfied.

"Well done," she said. "How would it be if we added the golden fillet?"

"I think that would be just the thing, my lady. A very good idea."

So Esther opened the jewel coffer and took out the

fillet: a slender band of gold set with tiny pearls. This she placed on Molly's head, low over the brow as a crown is worn.

"There!" she said. "How beautiful you look! No one would ever even dream that you've been ill."

"Well, I certainly look less a toad and more a swan," Molly said. "And all of it thanks to you. Now if you wouldn't mind, I'd like a bit of time alone to gather my wits."

"Of course, my lady."

"And will you take a message to Tobias?"

"*Lord Worthington*, my lady?"

"Yes. Please ask Lord Worthington to come to me as soon as we sail into port. I'm not very steady on my feet, I'm afraid, and I'll require his strong arm as we leave the ship."

"I will, my lady."

Molly would require a great deal more from Tobias than just his strong arm. What lay ahead of them now would be as hard for her as it was crucial for Westria. And for the thousandth time she thanked the stars that she had Tobias by her side.

⚜

When Esther had gone, Molly set the bolt in the door, pulled the canvas over the porthole, and settled herself on the only chair in the cabin. She closed her eyes—more out of habit than necessity, as the room was already dark—then, bit by bit, she released the tension from her face, her neck, her shoulders and arms, and on down to her feet till she had melted into the chair, soft and still.

Now, as she'd been taught, she emptied her mind of everything—the sickroom smell of the tight little cabin, the quiet rhythm of her heartbeat, the soft lap of waves against the hull—and focused on one thing only: moving deep down into her spirit-self in search of the vision of the future she so desperately needed but which had stubbornly refused to come.

This was something new for Molly, a skill she'd only learned the year before. Until that time she'd been at the mercy of her "Gift." She could neither summon the magical visions, nor could she make them go away. They just came when they wanted to. And they were unfailingly gruesome (no happy children dancing among the wildflowers, just unrelenting horror and death). As a result, Molly had lived for years in a constant state of anxiety, like a lonely traveler on a desolate road who knows that at any moment a cutthroat might suddenly appear and fall on her with a knife.

But then Alaric had sent her to Austlind, where

Molly's grandfather had lived and worked as a silversmith. He had been famous for the beautiful Loving Cups he made: silver chalices with the power to join two people in a bond of perfect love. That's what Alaric had wanted her to find: a magical cup to help him win the hand of the princess of Cortova, and with it the alliance his kingdom so desperately needed.

In this Molly had succeeded. The Loving Cup she'd brought back from Austlind now rested in Alaric's stateroom, bound for Cortova and the role it would play in great matters of state. But the journey itself had altered the course of her life.

The search for the cup had led her into the barren northlands of Austlind, where the secret walled city of Harrowsgode lay hidden behind a range of impenetrable mountains. This was her grandfather's birthplace, the ancestral home of Molly's people, and the source of her mysterious powers—for all Harrowsgode folk had the Gift to a greater or lesser degree.

But Molly's was unaccountably stronger than theirs. Indeed, only a handful of Magi, going back to the days of old King Magnus, had possessed such remarkable powers. Once she fully understood how to use them, she was destined to be truly great.

Many things had happened in Harrowsgode, not all of them good. But when Molly left the city (how and why she left is another story), she was well on her way to learning how to control her wayward Gift. She knew how to reach down to the depths of her inner spirit and find the things she wanted. A lesson like that was worth a lot of suffering.

Now she planned to use that knowledge to find a window into the future—because so far her wonderful Gift had sent her nothing but dark premonitions and a talking cat, which weren't nearly enough.

Molly knew from experience that danger could take many forms, and it would really be helpful to know what they were up against. For that matter, she didn't even know who was threatened. She'd assumed it was Alaric, but that had been lazy thinking. The premonition of terrible tragedy and the cat's suspicions about Gonzalo and Reynard might be two entirely different things. So it could be anyone, even Molly herself.

She had to know more. She focused her mind and made ready.

It was always a fearful thing, descending into that ever-changing shadow world. She had to steel herself every time just to bear it. She never knew what would happen down there, except that it would be a struggle. The Gift didn't give as freely as its name suggested it should. She had to go in there and take it.

On this particular day she found herself in a void,

utterly empty of movement or light. The air was stifling; it pressed against her and robbed her of breath. It felt like being trapped in a coffin buried far underground. There was nothing to see, nothing to feel, and only a single sound: the regular, heavy breathing of some great, sleeping beast.

It came to Molly that the sound wasn't coming from the other side of some invisible door or even from down below. It was everywhere. It surrounded and filled her so that she could actually feel the rumbling vibrations of each and every breath.

She was *inside* the beast.

No, she realized. It was worse than that. She *was* the beast. Or rather, the beast *was part of her spirit*—dormant now but filled with deadly potential. A thrill of terror ran through her body as she grasped this—and suddenly she could not, *could not* bear to stay there a moment longer.

Swimming up through the stifling gloom, she panicked and found that she couldn't catch her breath. It was like drowning, her chest tight and burning, crying out for air. And then at last she surfaced into the dim light of a small, stuffy cabin on a gently rolling ship.

Molly sat there for some time, heaving and trembling, cursing herself for a coward.

She had failed.

❊ 7 ❊

Tobias

TOBIAS AND MOLLY RODE side by side in the middle of the caravan in company with those few married knights who'd brought along their ladies. He couldn't help but notice the intimate quality of their conversations—the easy, familiar way they had of being together, sometimes speaking in a sort of couples' code, leaving sentences unfinished or things unsaid because they were already understood. They seemed to know automatically what the other would like to eat, where he or she would prefer to sit at dinner, or what would be of interest along the way. If they had nothing particular to say, they would ride in comfortable silence for hours. And whether or not they were truly fond, they seemed as easy together as they would have been alone.

He and Molly were like that too—not because they were married, which of course they weren't, but because they'd grown up together, had saved Alaric from the wolves together, and on several occasions had come very close to dying together. That sort of history builds intimacy and trust.

Though Tobias didn't know about Harrowsgode (only Alaric did), he knew most everything else, including Molly's vision of the cat and her concerns for Alaric's safety. He'd taken it seriously; she was never wrong about such things. So he'd been keeping a watchful eye out for anything suspicious, whether on the road or at the inns where they stopped for the night. And being of an analytical mind, he'd made a mental list of situations likely to arise in Cortova that were especially fraught with danger.

And yet, for all that, he couldn't *feel* what Molly felt—that deep disquiet, that presentiment of danger, which hung over her night and day. In fact, it seemed to Tobias that things were going uncommonly well. And that was hardly surprising, since Alaric had left nothing to chance. He might have *invaded* Cortova with less preparation than he'd put into this ceremonial visit.

Every member of their party had been chosen with special care. The court gentlemen who accompanied the king were all prominent knights, young enough and strong enough to do serious damage with their swords should serious damage with swords be required. Even the pages and squires who attended them had been handpicked by the master of arms. In addition, the king had brought along his physician, a lawyer to advise him on the terms of the contract, a linguist fluent in Cortovan, and a number of servants who weren't actually servants but spies.

Tobias, however, had none of these skills. So the others—most especially the highborn knights— wondered why on earth he'd been included. The lad was nothing but a cooper's son. And as recently as the previous year he'd worked in the king's stables, mucking out stalls, rubbing down horses, and scraping mud off gentlemen's boots.

And the knights remembered it too. Tobias stood out from the other lads because he was so very tall, with those broad shoulders and that shock of straw-colored hair. Indeed, he was overall such a remarkable specimen of manly grace that the wags among them had taken to calling him "the young Goliath," as in "Send for the young Goliath to unload that wagon."

Then just last year the king had rewarded him—for

some service or other, they didn't know what—by giving him a title by royal decree and a landed estate to go with it. But that was nothing but perfume on a pig. "Lord Worthington" was still just a stable boy, not even trained to be a common foot soldier. So why the king should insist on bringing the fellow to Cortova was beyond their imagining.

As it happened, he had a very good reason, and it was as follows:

Alaric had to bring Molly. He depended on her special powers to guide him and warn him of danger. They would often be seen together, and there was really no way of hiding their mutual regard. This presented a problem. Since Molly was pretty, young, and unmarried, Alaric was afraid that King Gonzalo might misconstrue their relationship—and that would not be at all helpful in winning the princess's hand. Molly must seem to be attached to somebody else.

With this in mind, Alaric had called Tobias back to court with no explanation, just the request that he bring his friend Lord Richard. Immediately upon their arrival they'd been ushered into the king's reception chamber, where Molly was already waiting, along with Winifred, her old chum from their days in service. Alaric had then dismissed his servants, even his guards, ordering them to wait outside.

"Forgive me, Tobias," he'd said, "but before the priest arrives, I must explain that we've created a little deception here."

The priest? What priest? Tobias had looked questioningly at Molly, but she was staring down at her shoes.

"He will bless our journey, and pray for a good outcome, and so forth."

Ah. But then why were he and Richard there? And Winifred?

"However, the court shall believe—and the priest will not say otherwise—that he was called for another purpose: to hear"—he'd taken a deep breath—"your vows of betrothal."

Tobias gasped. Molly cleared her throat. Neither had looked the other in the eye.

"If anyone asks, you will say that the wedding is set for a year from now, when Molly comes of age. I have rings for both of you to wear. Once the journey is over, of course, you can take them off again, and we'll spread the word that the betrothal was broken by mutual consent. We'll think up some good reason why."

Before Tobias could say a word—his mouth was already open—the king had held up a hand to stop him. "It had to be you, Tobias. No one else would be believed, and it's doubtful that anyone would even have been willing—"

Molly had shot the king a very hard look, and he'd left the rest unsaid.

"Are you?" Alaric asked. "Willing?"

Tobias was more than willing. Indeed, he'd have been glad to do the thing in earnest. But he said, "Your Grace, may I know the reason?"

"Of course. Your supposed betrothal to Molly will make it possible for her to travel with us, and often be seen at my side, without any suspicions that we are . . . in any way . . ."

"I understand. Yes, Your Highness, I will be glad to do whatever is needed."

"Thank you. Winifred and Richard, please make the point of mentioning that you witnessed the ceremony. Don't be too obvious about it, but spread the word. And Tobias, this means, of course, that you will have to come with us to Cortova. So I'll need you to stay on at court for your preparation. You'll be tutored in the language, as we all will; and I've asked the master of arms to take you under his wing—teach you a few basics of swordsmanship and hand-to-hand combat."

By this point Tobias had more or less lost the power of speech. So he'd simply nodded assent. Then, as everyone was now in agreement, the king went over to a table and opened a coffer such as jewelry is kept in. Inside were two small leather bags.

"I wasn't sure about the sizes," he'd explained, "so I had several rings made for each of you. One of them is bound to fit."

Rings, Tobias had thought. *Of course.*

The king had turned first to Molly, emptying the bag into his palm, then taking her left hand in his, studying it, selecting the right-sized ring, and slipping it onto her finger. Tobias couldn't have said why this bothered him so much, but the king certainly hadn't *needed* to do it that way—as if . . . well, as if *he* were being betrothed to her himself.

Then Alaric had handed Tobias the other bag, letting him choose his own ring, whichever fit best; and shortly thereafter the priest had arrived to ask God's blessing on the journey.

Thus it was that Tobias and Molly had become a couple in the eyes of the world.

Yet nothing between them had really changed. They continued to work together to do the king's bidding, to keep him safe, and to help him accomplish what he must for the good of Westria. They spoke to each other in couples' code, as old friends do, and anticipated each other's needs and thoughts. They rode side by side in companionable silence when there was nothing to say, and they laughed at jokes that no one else understood. They watched ravens circling overhead with special meaning. And they left important things unsaid because that's how Molly liked it, and it was how they'd always been with each other.

And yet, somehow, every time Tobias removed his gloves, or reached for a slice of bread, or washed his hands, it thrilled him to see that ring on his finger—though it meant nothing, of course. He knew that. It was just a very expensive prop in a little play they were acting out.

And yet . . .

Part Two

Development—the moving of pieces to new positions where their mobility and activity are increased.

Trap—a plan for tricking your opponent into making a losing move.

Day Two

❦ 8 ❧

It Gives Me the Shivers

THE GUEST COMPOUND OF the summer palace looked like an ancient village, with many freestanding houses, all in the antique style. Every guest villa had four to six sleeping chambers, a dining porch, a sitting room, a service pantry, a water-cleaned privy that didn't stink, a bathing room with a large pool fed by natural hot springs, and its own staff of slaves to see to the guests' every need. The bedrooms were handsomely furnished, each with a large bowl of flowers on the table, a platter of fruit, and a jug of wine. And since all of them opened onto a private central garden, they were wonderfully airy and bright.

King Alaric's villa was larger and more luxurious than the rest—though it was just as unremarkable from the outside, with its red-tile roof, white-plaster walls, and very little else besides a row of high, barred windows and the single entry door where Molly now stood, hesitating.

There was no telling who would answer her knock, though it would probably be Heptor Brochton. He was the senior knight on this journey, and his chief duty was to see to Alaric's safety. He seemed to think this included keeping the wrong sort of people—that is to say, Molly—as far away from the king as possible.

Lord Brochton was of royal lineage, his grandfather having been the younger brother of old King Mortimer, making him a distant cousin of the king. He was naturally proud of this connection. But due to a cascading string of misfortunes, Heptor had been born the second son of the second son of a second son. And so, because of the law of primogeniture (which required that all lands and titles go to the eldest son so as not to break up great estates by dividing them with each subsequent generation), Heptor had inherited nothing at all but sharp wits, abundant courage, and a strong right arm. These he'd used to such advantage in the reign of King Godfrey the Lame that Heptor had won for himself the lands and fortune he'd been denied at birth. He was now so highly respected that only King Alaric and Lord Mayhew stood above him. Lord Brochton was rightfully proud of this as well.

But like many a self-made man, he was a terrible snob; and he had taken a particular dislike to Molly. He thought it unseemly that the king of Westria should allow such a common, ignorant girl into his circle of friends; and he did all he could to keep them apart.

Molly was quite aware of this, of course—Lord Brochton made no effort (except when the king was around) to hide his disdain—and it made her uncomfortable. So now as she knocked on the door to Alaric's villa, she found herself hoping against hope that somehow, for some reason, Lord Brochton would be busy elsewhere and some other, kinder person would answer the door.

She heard the clump of boots growing louder as someone approached, and she cursed herself for a weakling as her heart slammed hard against her ribs. *Oh, for heaven's sake,* she thought; what was the worst the man could do to her? Sneer? Curl his lip?

The door opened.

"Yes?" Lord Brochton said.

"I wish to have a word with the king," she said.

"I'm afraid he's occupied."

"Then I'll wait. You might want to *tell* him I'm waiting, though."

This was a threat and not such a subtle one that Heptor couldn't grasp it. Alaric had made it abundantly clear that Molly was his trusted friend and very important to their mission. To send her away, or keep her waiting needlessly, or in any way treat her with contempt would make the king very angry.

"Of course," he said, still blocking the door and giving her a cold-eyed stare. "You can wait in the sitting room. I'll let him know you're here." Then reluctantly he moved aside. She slid past him with all the dignity she could muster.

When Alaric, having been informed of her presence, came directly out into the atrium—with his doublet off and his shirt hanging loose (he'd been undressing)—Molly noticed with some satisfaction how deeply this wounded the knight. When the king then invited her into his chamber rather than meet with her in a public space, Heptor had to turn his head away to hide his disgust.

Alaric sent his servants out, then scooped up the various articles of clothing that were lying on one of the chairs and tossed them onto the bed.

"Sit," he said, pulling over a second chair and setting it down beside hers. "I was hoping you'd come."

"There's a lot—"

"Yes, there is. Tell me what you think."

"I don't like it," she said. "It gives me the shivers."

"It gives me the shivers, too. I'd heard Gonzalo was a bit eccentric—wearing togas and all that. But I never expected a buffoon. Everything he said and did was peculiar, not at all appropriate or according to custom. And I rather think it was intentional. Did you notice how much he seemed to enjoy our discomfort? He was like some nasty little boy tearing wings off flies."

Molly didn't speak right away. She was still forming her thoughts.

"Yes," she finally said. "It was impossible to miss how much he enjoyed it. And I agree that he did it on purpose—to confuse and disarm you so you'll be at a disadvantage in discussing the terms. But Alaric, there's something else."

"Something more than that?"

She nodded. "That business about the summer palace having no great hall and his dining porch only accommodating nine, so unfortunately there will be no banquet—"

"That was a boldfaced lie, you know. He holds banquets here all the time—outdoors, on some terrace that overlooks a garden. That's what I've heard."

"My very point, Alaric. He knows you have spies,

same as he does. He knows you know he's spinning a tale, which means he *meant* to insult you. And more troubling still, this 'intimate little dinner' to which you can only bring two guests while the rest of your party must stay behind and eat in the guest quarters—"

"Incredibly rude."

"No, no, Alaric—*think*! It means you can only bring two of your knights. You'll be in a small space, under his control, practically alone—and then, and then—" She got up from her chair and went over to the bed, where a beautiful toga and mantle lay in the tangle of clothes. "He gives us these ridiculous costumes like his ancestors used to wear—"

"I told you; it's the custom here."

"I know. And they're exquisite, even mine. I'm sure they cost him a fortune. But look at this thing! It's as light as a spider's web and will offer you just as much protection. You might as well go naked to his little dinner."

"I see."

She dropped the toga and returned to her seat.

"Alaric," she said, "I'll only ask this once, then I'll never mention it again: Couldn't we just leave— right now, this afternoon? Go back to Westria and find some *other* princess to get you an heir, and trust Lord Mayhew to go on strengthening your forces and keeping you safe from Reynard's—"

"No."

"You feel safe here? You trust King Gonzalo with your life?"

"You promised not to mention it again."

"I'm not done mentioning it the first time."

"All right then, finish. Tell my why, after all our planning and considering everything we stand to gain here, you think we should turn tail and run. Have you seen a vision that portends my death?"

She paused. It would be such an easy and convenient lie. But she couldn't do it. "No," she said. "Not exactly."

"Not even another visit from the cat?"

"Well, yes. But there was nothing—"

"What did he say?"

She sighed. "That in the game of chess, the queen is the most powerful piece on the board."

"That's it?"

"Yes. Not helpful. But Alaric, sometimes I know things in a general way—not spelled out clearly in a vision but powerfully strong all the same. And I've been feeling this terrible dread. I told you about it on the ship, remember? Only now that we're actually here—" She balled her hands into fists and pressed them together, her body tense with the effort to find words to describe it. "It's worse, Alaric. I feel death. I feel loss. It's overwhelming, and it's real."

He sat back in his chair and took his time before responding.

"Molly, I've been thinking about what we discussed before, about how Gonzalo might already have made an arrangement with Reynard, one that includes my death. That troubled me a lot at first. But then I thought about it some more and decided it didn't make sense.

"Now, to answer to your question of a moment ago, *of course* I don't trust King Gonzalo—except to act in his own interest. And if I were killed, Reynard would inherit Westria and combine it with Austlind into one immensely powerful kingdom, right on the northern border of Cortova. That wouldn't benefit Gonzalo; it would turn Reynard into a threat. Don't you see? Whatever we have to fear from him, it most certainly isn't my death."

"It sounds reasonable. But it's not what I'm feeling. I'm feeling death."

"As you said. But I can't do it, Molly; I'm sorry. I can't just turn around and leave. I'd look a fool, and I'd lose my chance, and I'd be a laughingstock—"

"Oh, you're impossible."

He shrugged.

"Look—you brought me here to advise you, claiming to trust my Gift. That being the case, then my foreboding ought to balance out your logic. So be careful tonight. Keep your wits about you, and for heaven's sake, bring your best knights. Brochton for sure, plus Merrywell. Or maybe Janson."

"No. I want you and Tobias."

"Why, Alaric? That's insane!"

"Because if you're right, if danger is approaching, then a timely warning from you will be of far more use to me than a couple of knights who've left their swords behind, as courtesy demands."

"Then bring me *and* Lord Brochton."

"You know I can't do that. It wouldn't look right."

"In case you weren't aware of it, Alaric, being a king doesn't make you immortal."

"I had heard that, but I dismissed it as an ugly rumor."

"At least forget the toga and wear your doublet, with chain mail underneath."

"That would offend my host."

"God's breath but you're stubborn! Will you bring the cup?"

"No. Not yet. I want to get the lay of the land first,

see what other surprises the good Gonzalo has in store for us. I wouldn't put it past him not to bring the princess at all."

"Surely—"

"I'll grant it's unlikely, but no more so than having us to dinner in the palace kitchen."

"Not the kitchen."

"You take my meaning. And I certainly don't want to come bearing a gift for the princess only to have her father take it instead, promising to give it to her on the morrow."

"You're right. He might take a fancy to it and keep it for himself—you know, for enjoying a nice little cup of chilled wine on a hot afternoon."

"Heaven help us, Molly—what a hideous thought! Do you suppose I would then have to marry horrible old King Gonzalo?"

Suddenly it all seemed terribly funny and they laughed till they were almost sick. It felt good. It broke the tension.

But after a while, when Alaric had regained his kingly composure, Molly went on laughing, unable to control herself. The laughter just kept coming, wave after wave of it, till her face was red and her cheeks were wet with tears.

"Molly, stop," Alaric said then, his voice sharp.

But she couldn't. She slipped off the chair and onto the floor, where she knelt, her face buried in her hands. Still the laughter came in spasms, only now its character had changed. It was as if a dam inside her had given way, and all the emotions that had been building up inside were pouring out. She felt lighter for having shed them, so light that she was half afraid she'd float away. But Alaric was holding her now, keeping her connected to the earth—though his arms gripped her rather too fiercely, as if he were restraining a wild and dangerous beast or a madwoman having a fit.

Finally she went limp, the laughter gone. But still they remained as they were: on the floor, Molly in his arms—except that now he held her gently, as a lover would, his head leaning against her neck, his hand stoking her hair.

And then she was crying.

And then it was over.

❦ 9 ❧

A Very Deep Game

SHORTLY AFTER SUNSET, SLAVES bearing lamps came to Alaric's villa to escort him and his companions to dinner. They formed a tight little procession, with two slaves in front and two behind to light their way, and the three of them in the middle. Alaric went ahead, looking quite handsome in his beautiful toga—handsome, small, and defenseless. Molly and Tobias followed close behind. All of them were as watchful as cats.

The palace, like most royal residences, was fortified with both an inner and an outer curtain wall. The outer wall was extensive, enclosing everything from the stables and craftsmen's workshops to the fishpond, the brewer's yard, and the guest compound. The much smaller inner wall protected the king's domain.

When the procession arrived at this inner wall, the gate was already open, a guard on either side standing at attention. But as soon as they'd passed through, it was shut behind them, its great iron bolt thrown with a harsh, metallic *clang*. The sound made Molly's skin crawl. It was a dark reminder that walls weren't just for keeping enemies out. Sometimes walls were for keeping people in.

They continued along a series of covered walkways lit by torches on the walls, turning first one way, then another, until finally they reached a large courtyard garden. This Molly recognized. They'd been there earlier in the day, shortly after they'd arrived. But it had looked completely different then.

Candles now lined the paths and marked the edge of the pool, while the rest of the garden, with its wealth of flowers and ornamental shrubs, lay shrouded in darkness. And the dining porch, which she hadn't even noticed before, was ablaze with little lamps—the light glinting off the gold frames of the dining couches, casting its warm glow over the ancient frescoes on the walls, picking up the sheen of purple silk cushions, and spilling out onto the walkway beyond, right to the garden's edge.

Suddenly Alaric came to a halt and froze in a defensive posture: leaning forward, his hands slightly raised and away from his sides as if ready to draw a sword that wasn't there. At the same moment, Molly felt his fear pass over her like an icy draft from an open door. What had he seen that had caused him such alarm?

She squinted intently at the room—searching, searching—but nothing seemed the least bit threatening. The other six diners were already there, sitting on the benchlike couches: three and three, across from one another. And a few servants were bustling about, making last-minute preparations. But that was all.

Then something told her to look at the diners themselves.

From left to right she scanned the faces. First couch: a young boy, next to him King Gonzalo, and then the princess. Middle couch: empty, waiting for them. Third couch: older boy, vaguely familiar . . .

And then, for the second time that night, she felt the little hairs rise all over her skin. Because the next face she came to was more than vaguely familiar. It belonged to King Reynard of Austlind.

Tobias had spotted him too. He gasped and grabbed Molly's arm.

"I know," she whispered. Her mind was racing now, trying to put all the pieces together but finding that they didn't quite fit. Because if Alaric was wrong and the two kings really *were* colluding to murder him—maybe the plan was to split Westria between them—why show their hand so openly? It was careless and sloppy. And that didn't sound like Reynard.

Unless he had insisted on being there so he could watch his cousin die. Now, *that* Molly could believe. Because Alaric had been the innocent cause of the most shameful, humiliating failure of King Reynard's life.

It had been some time after the night of the wolves. The royal family of Westria had all been slain—except for Alaric, who had disappeared and was presumed to have drowned in the course of his escape. So Reynard had declared the prince dead, claimed the throne on legitimate grounds, and was already planning his coronation when along came Alaric, very much alive, riding down that hill to the walls of Dethemere Castle, followed by half the kingdom. And there he'd stood— just a boy, really, all of sixteen, with unkempt hair and slept-in clothes, his handsome face glowing like the sun—calling up to his cousin on the ramparts, asking Reynard to open the gates and acknowledge him as the rightful king of Westria.

Reynard had laughed.

It was Molly who'd given Alaric the idea that had

sent his cousin packing. It had been clever, and it had worked. But that victory had come at a heavy price because Reynard, like any wounded animal, was far more dangerous now. For a proud man to have been bested by a boy young enough to be his own son, to have been frightened away by some story about a family curse so that he'd run home to Austlind with his tail between his legs—oh, how that must have chafed at his spirit this past eighteen months and more. How deep and bitter must his hatred have grown!

Yes, Reynard would want to be there to see the knife go in. He might even wish to do the deed himself.

"Your Grace?" It was one of the slaves, who didn't understand why they had stopped. "Please, won't you come? My lord King Gonzalo is waiting."

"Of course," Alaric said.

⚜

As they emerged from the darkness of the garden into the light from the porch, Gonzalo leaped up from his couch and came out to greet them, his arms outstretched like a fond uncle.

"Welcome, welcome!" he cried. "Isn't this a grand evening? Come—join the party!"

But Molly wasn't paying attention to their host; she

was still staring at Reynard—and so she saw the look of horror cross his face. That's when the pieces finally fell into place, and everything made sense: Reynard wasn't in collusion with King Gonzalo; he *hadn't even known* Alaric was coming! The king of Cortova had brought them both there to *compete* for the prize—sort of an auction, with the princess and the alliance going to the highest bidder.

Gonzalo was making introductions now, as smoothly and graciously as if he actually liked them and really expected them to like each other.

"Son," he said to the handsome boy who sat on the end of the couch, furiously kicking his legs back and forth. "Stand up. That's it. I want you to meet King Alaric of Westria. This is my son, Prince Castor."

The boy nodded in an offhand way; it was hardly a bow at all—certainly not what was appropriate when greeting a king. At the same time he did something disdainful with his nose: flaring the nostrils as if he detected a stink. Watching this, Molly felt herself drawn back to her childhood on the streets, and her hackles went up as they always had when she was challenged by a bully. In those days she'd have used her fists. Now she just squinted her eyes at the child, slightly baring her upper teeth. He saw it and blinked with surprise.

"And this lovely creature—I'm sure you've already guessed—is my daughter, Princess Elizabetta. Of course you know King Reynard and Prince Rupert, though perhaps not Lord Wroxton, the king's friend." (He was actually the king's bodyguard, but it would have been rude to state the obvious.) "And I believe this is Lady Marguerite and her husband, Lord Worthington?"

"Not husband," Alaric corrected. "They are only betrothed."

"Ah. My mistake. Not yet married. Well, who knows? Perhaps a double wedding is in the stars!"

It hadn't been "his mistake," of course. It had been quite intentional. And Molly had the feeling it was meant to wound—though what Gonzalo hoped to accomplish by it was impossible to guess. Maybe it had just been a lead-in for the remark about the "double wedding," in which the identity of the *other* couple was yet to be determined. A bit subtler and more elegant than "Let the games begin!"

Gonzalo now returned to his couch and proceeded to make himself comfortable: reclining at an angle, turned halfway on his side, one arm draped over a large silk bolster. The others waited till the king was settled, then followed suit.

Alaric had been placed at the end of the middle

couch, directly beside the princess. This seemed such a blatant mark of favor that Molly shot a glance at Reynard to see how he was taking it. But she learned nothing. His face was a blank. So she turned her attention back to Alaric.

He and the princess were deep in conversation. She was leaning in toward him, her face transformed by a radiant smile, her eyes bright with interest. Then, in a flash, her expression altered, as though the clouds had moved in and obscured the sun. She reached over and took Alaric's hand in a consoling sort of way.

"I know," Molly heard her say in a voice that was soft and deep. "I know."

The princess gave Alaric's hand a squeeze, then released it. Molly watched, fascinated, as the sun slowly began to emerge from the clouds once again.

"I was glad when Father told me that you had . . . enquired about me. I . . ." She blushed and glanced down, then looked shyly up again.

"I was afraid that the very idea of a connection with me might be painful for you."

"It was. It . . . it still is, a little." She smiled sheepishly. "But at the same time, I know you understand my feelings in a way that others could not. We shared the same tragedy—though of course it was worse for you, as he was your brother."

"I suppose that's true."

"Edmund was terribly fond of you, you know, so eager for us to meet and like each other. He said— What was it? Let me think—that you were one of the few people in the world he trusted without question. He said you were doggedly loyal to those you loved and loyal to your ideals—though perhaps a little too saintly."

Alaric laughed. "*Saintly*—oh, my! I'm afraid my brother was wrong about that. I was a self-righteous little prig, if you want to know the truth. I do hope I've grown out of it by now."

"I hope so too," she said, raising her brows and grinning.

A little girl now came into the dining porch dressed in sky-blue silk and carrying a basket in her hands. With the delicate grace of a tiny dancer, she scattered rose petals onto the tables, then quietly tiptoed away.

Moments later there came a blast of trumpets as the slaves brought in the basin, the ewer, and the towels. As at any banquet in any great hall, they went first to the king, who held his hands above the bowl as perfumed water was poured over them, then dried them with a fine linen cloth. Likewise, according to rank, the rest of the royal family and their guests did the same.

And then the little sprite was back again, silver bells in each of her hands. She tinkled them sweetly as she led a procession of waiters into the room. They held their golden platters high, like offerings to the gods; and the dining porch was filled with an incense of cinnamon, cardamom, turmeric, and cloves.

Rich and elaborate dishes were expected at a royal dinner, but these were exotic and new. They came bathed in sauces that bit the tongue and excited the senses. They whispered of faraway lands: of camel caravans laden with silks and spices making their way across scorching desert sands, and of colorful markets bustling with noise and color, where men wore turbans and mangoes were sold, and pomegranates, coconuts, and dates.

This was to be a culinary tour of the world, a reminder that Cortova was not some insular, landlocked kingdom. Gonzalo practically owned the Southern Sea. The world lay at his feet within easy reach of his famous fleet of trading ships. And an alliance with all that wealth and power was theirs to gain or lose.

Molly thought yet again that they'd best not underestimate this man. He played a subtle game, and he played it very well. Nothing would ever be as simple as it seemed.

"Do you hunt?" the princess asked, her voice very soft now. The buzz of conversation had dropped since the food came in.

"On occasion," Alaric said. "I'm no sportsman, but I'm rather good with a bow. You'd never think it to look at me." Then, with a wicked grin, "My cousin Reynard deserves all the credit. I was fostered with him as a boy and was trained by his master of arms."

"I was aware of that, yes." The princess pinched her lips and met his wicked smile with one of her own. "I suppose this is all rather awkward for you."

"You might say that."

"Well, you'll have a chance to show your prowess very soon. Father has arranged a hunt for later in the week."

"Will you be riding out?"

"Of course. I wouldn't miss it for the world."

"Then I shouldn't have boasted. Now I'll have to prove myself."

"Indeed you will. I promise to stare at you constantly and make you nervous."

Molly smiled down at her hands, finding that she rather liked this princess and noting with some satisfaction that things were going remarkably well. Not only had they not been murdered, which was certainly a relief, but Alaric seemed to be running well ahead of poor Prince Rupert in the race to win the princess's heart.

Everything they'd done this past year and more had been leading up to this very moment. And suddenly it felt very real. The princess wasn't just some prize to be won; she was an actual flesh-and-blood girl. And if everything went as planned, she would soon be Alaric's wife. She would share his bed, give him sons, and rule the kingdom at his side. She'd become his dearest friend, privy to his most intimate secrets. And she'd be his helpmate, too, sharing the burdens of office he had heretofore carried alone. Alaric, having expected nothing beyond the usual royal marriage—which would bring him an alliance and, with any luck, an heir—would be overcome with gratitude that such a treasure should be his. Doubly bound by the harmony of their natures and the magic of the Loving Cup, they would grow closer and fonder as each day passed till at last they'd achieved that rarest of feelings: a truly perfect love.

It was more than she could possibly have hoped—for Alaric and for Westria. It would be a real, rays-of-sunlight-streaming-from-the-clouds, swelling-music, showering-apple-blossoms kind of happy ending.

"Lady Marguerite?"

The words drifted into Molly's consciousness like a leaf blown by the wind. She looked up and saw that the waiters had cleared away the platters and were now setting down little silver cups filled with iced fruit. And the princess was gazing expectantly at Molly with one of those radiant smiles that she had heretofore reserved for Alaric.

"I'm sorry, Your Highness—were you speaking to me?"

"I was, but you seemed lost in thought. I hope I didn't interrupt something profound."

"Not at all. Just woolgathering, I'm afraid. What were you saying?"

"I asked whether you played chess."

Molly stared in astonishment.

"Chess," she said stupidly, struggling to regain her composure. "Why no, I never have. But how very strange—I've been thinking of late how much I'd like to learn."

"Really? Well, then I shall teach you! I'll get to enjoy your company, and I'll feel so frightfully clever when I beat you—which of course I will at first. But then, once you've mastered the game, we can battle it out; and that'll be even more fun. What do you say?"

"That's very kind, Your Highness. I'd be greatly honored."

"Good. I'll send for you tomorrow then. In the morning."

"Thank you. I'll be ready."

Molly couldn't help wondering what the princess would think if she knew that her new friend, "the lady Marguerite," had once scrubbed pots in the palace kitchen. Would she smile so sweetly on Molly then? Would she still expect to "enjoy her company"?

And then it hit her with the force of a blow: the princess *already knew*.

Well, *of course* she did! Gonzalo had spies all over Westria, where Molly's story was common knowledge: the scullion who'd been raised to high station and now went about in silk and jewels. It was just the sort of delicious gossip that King Gonzalo would appreciate, and there was no way he wouldn't have shared it with his daughter.

Assuming she knew, and considering that no princess would really want to spend time with someone like Molly, the only obvious conclusion was that she was doing her father's bidding, acting as Gonzalo's spy.

So it had all been false: Elizabetta's kind invitation, those warm smiles and sweet words, possibly even her attentions to Alaric. Just part of a very deep game.

And suddenly a different version of the future played out in Molly's imagination. Alaric would still be seduced by Elizabetta's beauty and the power of the Loving Cup. She'd still be his queen, and share his bed, and give him sons. But his mind would know better than to trust her. She'd never be the partner of his life. He would carry his burdens alone and keep his secrets to himself. His marriage would be exactly what he'd expected from the start: an arrangement based on property, politics, and the need for an heir to the throne—and nothing more.

At last the dinner was over. Slaves were assembling and lighting their lamps, preparing to lead the guests back to their quarters for the night. Only then did King Gonzalo get down to business.

"My lord king Alaric," he said, "I will send for you in the morning to discuss the matter at hand. Then, it is the custom here in Cortova to rest during the hottest part of the day. But I should be ready to receive *you*, my lord king Reynard, in the cool of the late afternoon. Will that be acceptable? Good.

"So then, dear friends, I bid you farewell until we meet tomorrow."

Once again they formed a procession, with two slaves in front and two behind to light their way. Once again Alaric walked alone, followed by Molly and

Tobias. And once again they crossed the garden on a path marked by shimmering candles.

They had almost reached the covered walkway on the far side of the atrium when they caught a sudden movement in the darkness. Something had dashed out from behind a hedge and darted in front of them; then having reached the safety of a flowerbed, it sat and looked up very pointedly at Molly.

"Don't be alarmed, Your Highness," said the slave who was in the lead. "That's just the princess Elizabetta's cat. We call him Leondas, because he's half as big as a lion."

"Was that—?" Tobias whispered in Molly's ear.

"Yes," she said. "It was."

Day Three

❦ 10 ❧

Like Father,
Like Daughter

"I WANT IT IN writing," she said. "Two copies. One for me and one for you, both with your privy seal."

"You don't trust me to keep my word?"

The princess laughed. "Of course I don't. Nor can I assume that you'll die in your bed surrounded by scribes busily taking notes as you put your affairs in order. You might die suddenly. And if there's no official document attesting to the change of heirs, then where will I be?"

"Goodness—who laid *your* egg in my nest?"

"Why, you did, Father. How can you doubt it? Just look at me and you'll see yourself, only younger and much more attractive."

He did look at her then, in a studying sort of way, scratching his neck at the hairline right behind the left ear. It was an old, unconscious habit of his, something he did when he was nervous. The princess took note of it.

"We made a bargain, Father, and so far I've kept my part. But I want assurance in writing that you'll keep yours. If you refuse, then I will not only stop being charming—I will actively work against you in every possible way. And if you think I can't send them packing, then you'd better think again."

"You don't become the heir until a treaty is signed. That was our agreement."

"Ah, but once a treaty is signed, I'll have lost my advantage."

He shrugged.

"Come now. Must I write out a draft for you? All you need say is: 'I hereby alter the royal succession in favor of my daughter, Princess Anna Maria Elizabetta, who shall rule the kingdom of Cortova upon my death, *conditional to* the signing of a satisfactory treaty of alliance with either the king of Westria or the king of Austlind.' See how easy that was?"

"Don't you have an engagement this morning? With Lady What's-her-name?"

"Don't worry. It can wait. We have all the time in the world. And how long can it really take to write out a few brief lines—and sign them, and seal them? Hmm?"

"I can't think why you'd want to play chess with a girl like that. She's nothing but a peasant."

"Really? And yet she holds the favor of a great king and is betrothed to a mighty lord."

"He's a peasant too—that so-called lord. King Alaric raised them up. It was the laughingstock of Westria for months."

"Well, Father, you do have a lot of information. I'll bet you could even call up the lady's name if you tried."

"I could. I merely meant to disparage her."

"Yes. I figured that out by myself. But I wonder, since you know so much about so many things, why you never thought to share any of it with me?"

"It's my business to know things. It's your business to look pretty, and be winning, and make sons."

"No, Father, not anymore. So please stop changing the subject and wasting time. Let's get our business done so I can go draw King Alaric's little peasant into my web, and you can go back to torturing our guests. Here is some parchment, and here is your pen. Shall I dictate?"

"That won't be necessary."

"I want to read it when you're done. Both copies."

He looked up at her, his eyes near closed to slits, serpentlike. "You *are* my chick," he said, dipping his pen into the inkwell. "How is it I didn't see the resemblance before?"

"You never bothered to notice. More fool, you."

He frowned and began to write in a beautiful, formal hand, as was fitting for such an important document. All the while he muttered to himself. "My stars, but you will surprise them—all those courtiers who'll assume you're weak because you're a woman and brainless because you're pretty. They'll try to use you and manage you through flattery. Huh! I wouldn't be in their shoes when they discover their mistake. No, I most definitely would not."

When he'd finished, the king handed his daughter the document. When she'd nodded approval, he began again, writing out a duplicate on a second sheet of parchment.

"A woman on the throne of Cortova!" he went on, still talking to himself. "What a spectacle that will be—like gladiators battling lions in the ring, only so much more original, you know, something no one has seen before. I'm just sorry I won't live to see it."

"That could be arranged."

The king laughed so hard that he blotted the

page and had to start over again. But Elizabetta never smiled, not once. She just stood beside her father's desk, following his pen with her eyes, scanning every word he wrote on the document that would one day make her queen of Cortova.

When King Gonzalo had signed both copies, he folded them into two neat packages. Then, with Elizabetta working the flint, he lit the wick of the sealing wax and held it over the first document, just at the tip of the final fold. Melting wax dropped onto the parchment like blood from a wound, forming a thick puddle, red and glistening. Gonzalo removed his signet ring, pressed the face of it into the wax, and held it there till the seal had cooled and hardened. When he took the signet out, the impression was sharp and clear: the Lion Shield of Cortova.

He sealed the second document in the same manner and gave one of the copies to his daughter.

"Was that so very hard?" she asked.

"What do you think?" He met her eyes with such a murderous look that it was all she could do not to flinch. "You just forced me to disinherit my son."

"Castor hasn't the making of a king, Father. You know it's true. He'd have destroyed everything you've built."

"You don't know that. He's still a child."

"He will *always* be a child."

"Go!" Gonzalo said suddenly, waving her away.

And when she didn't leave instantly—transfixed as she was by the anguish displayed so openly on his face, thinking that this was the most honest moment they'd ever shared—he raged at her. "I bleed!" he shouted, pressing his fist hard against his belly.

And she believed it.

❦ 11 ❧

A Safe and Secret Place

AS THE PRINCESS STEPPED out of the king's chamber into the hall, still trembling from what she'd just done, Elizabetta heard the scuffling sound of running feet. She squinted into the shadows but only caught the flash of a light-colored tunic as a figure rounded the corner.

At the same moment it occurred to her that there was no one guarding the door.

She stood, unmoving, for the briefest time, deciding what to do. She longed to give chase because she very much wanted to find out who had dared to eavesdrop on their conversation—and was now in possession of her dearest secret. But she knew the hallway led to a blind court: nothing but service rooms and slaves' quarters. No one would have run in that direction unless the intent was to draw her into a trap.

And the missing guard—where was he? Also waiting in the shadows at the end of the hall, his weapon drawn?

Her decision made, Elizabetta turned and ran the other way, cutting across the atrium, then racing down the long colonnade that led to the east end of the compound. Everyone she passed stared in astonishment as she flew by; but the princess ignored them, never slowing her pace until she'd reached the safety of her own chambers.

She sat on her bed, breathing hard and trembling. Giulia and Estella, seeing her distress, hovered like a little cloud of butterflies, asking if she was all right and was there anything they could do. But Elizabetta sent them away. She wanted only Claudia, her old and trusted servant.

Claudia had been in charge of the late queen's household for many years and before that had served her in lesser positions. Over the course of all that time the two had grown as easy and affectionate as sisters.

Shortly before her death, the queen had summoned Claudia to her side and released her from bondage.

Then she'd asked—*asked*—her friend and former slave for one last favor. Would she, dear Claudia, stay on at the palace as a paid servant and look after the little princess?

The old woman had broken down entirely then so that her answering words were lost amid the hiccups, gulps, and sobs. But the queen had understood her perfectly. This good soul, who had been at her side for as long as she could remember—offering wise advice when it was asked for, giving assurance and affection when it was wanted, and having the delicacy to fade into the background when she was not needed at all—would be there to protect and guide little Betta with that same tender care. Knowing this, she could die in peace.

Later that same night, in the deep silence of the small hours, the queen had departed this life. The priest had already gone by then, along with the crowd of courtiers. Only the king and Claudia had kept watch with her. But when death had finally come, Gonzalo had been asleep, his head lolling back against his chair. Only Claudia, who'd been holding her mistress's hand, knew the moment she was gone.

Elizabetta had never heard this story. Claudia was far too discreet to tell it. But if you'd asked the princess to imagine her mother's final breath, she would have come very close to the truth: Claudia would have been there; and she would have stayed awake through a month of long nights, if it had been called for, so her beloved mistress wouldn't have to die alone.

Thus it was natural, at this moment of crisis when nothing in the world seemed clear or certain and danger lurked in the shadows, that the princess should turn to Claudia, as she had so many times before.

"This," she said, holding up the sealed document, "is the most precious thing in my possession. I'll tell you what it is when we have time, but right now I need to hide it in a safe and secret place. I'll require your help, I'm afraid. We must move the bed."

"Of course," Claudia said.

It was heavy, made of gilded bronze, so they had to shift it bit by bit—heaving and resting, heaving and resting—till the bed was far enough away from the wall for the princess to slip in behind and pry up one of the tiles, revealing a hidden compartment. In it, carefully wrought to fit the space, was a sturdy iron box.

She'd found this secret hiding place many years before, at a time when the furniture was arranged in a different way and the loose tile hadn't been covered by anything heavy. It must have been there since the floor was first laid many centuries past. The princess had been enchanted by it, imagining all the secret treasures that had been hidden there over the years and making up stories about them.

When her little child's bed had been replaced by a large one, she'd been very particular about where it should be placed, making sure that one of the legs rested directly on the special tile. It was as if she'd known that one day she'd want to put something important there, and she didn't want anyone coming across it by accident, as she had.

Now that day had come. And she noted with pleasure that the document fitted perfectly, as if the box had been especially designed to hold it. Smiling, she closed the lid and replaced the tile, then scrambled over the bed. Once again they shifted it, in slow stages, till it was back against the wall. When Claudia had smoothed the coverlet and arranged the cushions, everything looked exactly as it had before.

"Now," said the princess, "I need a few minutes alone to catch my breath. Tell Giulia to set up the chessboard and lay out some refreshments. Then send a runner to fetch Lady Marguerite."

"Yes, my lady," Claudia replied.

She was about to go out, her hand already on the latch, when she turned and looked back at her mistress.

"You were so *very* like your lady mother just now,"

she said. "So strong and resourceful, I half thought the angels had brought her back to me."

"Claudia," the princess said, "that was the single thing in all the world I most needed to hear."

❦ 12 ❧

Black Queen/
White Queen

MOLLY HAD SEEN THE princess on three separate
occasions, and she'd been a different person each time.
In Westria, Elizabetta had been a grand lady, exotic
and yet familiar in her sumptuous gown and jewels.
Last night, at the dinner, her simple dress and manner had made her seem young and sweet, even more
beautiful than before. Now, as she greeted Molly in a
well-worn tunic not even as nice as the ones her slaves
were wearing, her hair braided loosely in back, much
of it escaping at the sides in wayward curls, her face
glowing and her expression bright with expectation,
Elizabetta was transformed yet again. Now she was

Molly's comfortable old friend—like Winifred, except that she was a princess, and beautiful.

The chessboard had been set up outside on the covered porch, where they could enjoy the garden as they played. They sat on gilded chairs on either side of the table, facing each other.

Molly had seen people play chess before. She even had a board of her own back at Barcliffe Manor. It had come with the estate (along with the books she couldn't read and the instruments she couldn't play). But none of the sets she'd seen in the past, even including Alaric's, could compare with what lay before her now.

Everything white was made from ivory, and everything black was ebony. The pieces, which were uncommonly large, were like miniature statues, beautifully carved with all sorts of intricate details. One of them—a woman wearing a wimple and a crown—was seated on a throne. She leaned forward, her chin resting on her right palm, her left hand clasping her right elbow. You could see the folds of her robe and the embroidery on it. Even the back of her throne was intricately carved in a swirling pattern of leaves and vines. But what struck Molly in particular was the way you could almost *feel* her thinking—something very serious, very deep.

"These pieces are so beautiful," she said, "it almost

seems a shame to play with them."

"Yes, they are beautiful," the princess agreed. "And very old, as so many things in this palace are. But I assure you; they're also quite fun to play with. Because they're so lifelike, you come to feel a kind of sympathy for them. And as you move them about the board and give them adventures, you will rejoice at their triumphs and grieve when they fall."

"I can see how that would be so."

"Indeed. Shall we begin?"

"Yes, Your Highness. Please."

The princess shot her one of those apparently false but disarming smiles, then chose a piece from the back row and held it up for Molly to see. It was a figure of a bearded man, also wearing a crown. He was seated, and he held a sword across his knees, the hilt in his right hand, his left touching the point of the blade. His eyes were wide, as if he were startled.

"This is the king," the princess said. "If you lose your king, you lose the game."

She set down the piece and took up the thoughtful lady who was also in the back row and who sat beside the king.

"And this, of course, is the queen. She's the most powerful piece you have."

"But why would the queen be more powerful than

the king? It isn't that way in real life." Then Molly remembered her manners and added, "Your Royal Highness."

"Oh, please! We're not at court, and I'd hoped we could be friends. Call me Betta."

Molly resisted a strong inclination to believe that the princess was sincere.

"It would be an honor," she said.

"And in return, may I call you Marguerite?"

"You can call me whatever you like, but I'd rather you called me Molly."

"Is that how King Alaric addresses you?"

"Yes. Marguerite is the name I was given at birth, but I'm Molly to my friends."

"It suits you better, I agree. Now then, Molly, to answer your question, I'm not exactly sure why it's so. But I imagine the king is slow and deliberate because he's so busy, weighed down by his many responsibilities. And wherever he goes he has to take his court, and his guards, and his servants with him. His life is restricted by his greatness. Whereas the queen, well, we ladies are light on our feet, clever, and quick." She gave Molly a quick little grin. "We can work secretly, behind the scenes."

"Ah."

"Now, in keeping with the personalities of the

pieces, each one moves in a different way. Our poor king can only move one square at a time, though at least he can move in any direction he wants. But clearly he needs protecting."

"And the queen?"

"She can move as many squares as she wants and in any direction. That's why she's so powerful."

Molly nodded.

"Now, here's your bishop—see, he's wearing his miter, and holding his pastoral staff, and giving the sign of blessing? We each have two of them—only the king and queen are single pieces. And, like the queen, the bishops can go as far as they want—but only on the diagonal. Like this, across the corners of the squares. So we ladies are still superior.

"I know it's a lot to remember, Molly, but you'll catch on pretty quickly. And once you've learned, we can play every day—if you're willing."

Molly wondered just how long the princess thought they'd be staying in Cortova. Even with Reynard thrown into the mix, the negotiations shouldn't take more than a week. So was Betta saying, in a very guarded manner, that they would have years and years to play chess—after she had married Alaric and become queen of Westria?

"What about your ladies of the court? Don't any of them play chess?"

She shrugged. "A few. But they always let me win because they think that's what I want. And they're not what you'd call 'companions.' They're— Well, I have the feeling you know exactly what court ladies are."

Molly blinked. What did she mean by that?

"I'm a very good judge of character," the princess said, answering her unspoken question, "in case you were wondering how I knew. And I can plainly see that you're neither silly nor shallow. You're tough, and you're wise, and you're interesting. That's why I want you for my friend."

Molly was momentarily speechless. Were they still playing Gonzalo's game? Finally she stammered out the best reply she could manage, which also happened to be the truth. "I am overcome," she said.

"Well, you shouldn't be. I don't give my affections lightly, and I never say things I don't mean. If I have chosen to like and trust you, that's because I think you deserve it."

These words were so flattering that Molly really wanted to believe them. What's more, her instincts kept leading her on—urging her to return Betta's trust, to believe that the princess really wanted to be her friend, that she truly never said things she didn't mean, and that she posed no danger to Alaric.

Just then, as if in support of Molly's intuition, the cat came strolling into the atrium. He stopped and stared at Molly as he'd done the night before, then leaped onto Betta's lap, landing so heavily he made her gasp.

"Goodness but you're a monster," the princess said, scooting back her chair to give him a bit more room and waiting till he'd settled himself. "This is Leondas," she said. "He's adopted me, and everyone thinks that's very funny. He's such a common, ugly old cat, you know, and so extremely large."

"We've met, actually." Molly said. "In the garden, last night."

"Do you like cats?"

"Yes. This one in particular."

"Well, that's a relief, because I've grown unaccountably fond of him."

"It's because he's so interesting and wise. Probably tough as well."

Elizabetta laughed. "I knew I was right about you," she said. "Now pay attention. Your lesson isn't over yet. The next piece—I'll bet you can guess."

Molly studied it. The figure wore a helmet, carried a spear, and rode a very tiny horse. "He's a knight,"

Molly said, delighted. "A funny little knight."

"Exactly so. And like the bishop, you have two of them. But unlike the bishop, who's such a pious, proper sort of fellow—everything done according to the rules of doctrine—our knight must adapt himself to the constantly changing conditions of battle. So he never goes *straight at* anything; he moves in devious ways: one step forward and two to the side, or two steps forward and one to the side—in any direction. He can even leap over other pieces so long as he ends up on an empty square. See—like this. Or this. Or this. Understand?"

"Yes. I do."

"That's good, because if people are going to throw up their hands and say chess is too impossibly hard, you usually lose them with the knight."

A swallow darted in just then. They looked up and watched as it disappeared into the tangle of vines that had grown up the columns and along the beams of the atrium roof. Leondas watched it, too, with hunter's eyes.

"How long have you known King Alaric?" the princess asked.

Molly didn't quite know what to make of this sudden and direct change of subjects; but since it concerned Alaric, she went on the alert.

"Are you old friends?" Betta went on when Molly didn't reply. "He seems to hold you in especially high regard."

"We were children when we first met," Molly said. (This was true, but far from the whole truth. At the time, Molly had been a servant and Alaric a prince. He'd been passing through the great hall and had happened to notice that she was staring at him, not looking humbly down at her feet as lowly retainers were supposed to do. He'd responded by telling her, quite unpleasantly, to mind who she looked at—which by no definition of the word really counted as "meeting.") "But then he was sent away to Austlind. It was only after he came back that we became friends."

The princess watched her intensely, like a hawk studying its prey. "You are very fond of him," she said. It was a statement, not a question.

"He's my king. And my friend."

"I understand. And Lord Worthington? You are betrothed, I believe?"

She knew this, of course. It had been mentioned the night before.

"Yes. I have also known Tobias since I was a very little child."

"A love match, then?" She smiled at that.

"Yes, Your Majesty. And he well deserves my love,

for he is generous of heart, kind, clever, funny, and brave. He would give his life for me without a second thought."

The princess sucked in breath. "You are very fortunate, then."

"I am indeed."

"With royal marriages . . . well, one seldom has choices in matters of the heart."

Molly was blunt because she couldn't help it. "Are you asking me if Alaric is someone you could love and trust?"

Another gasp and a smile of astonishment. "You *are* direct," she said.

"Unspeakably rude, I'm afraid. Please accept my apology."

"I will not, for none is owed. Of course I would like to know what sort of man he is, as he has come here asking for my hand—beyond the obvious fact that he is handsome and that he can be quite charming when he wishes."

"Well, he is a great deal more than that—as I suspect you already know, as you are such a fine judge of character."

"But aren't we all a great deal more than we seem, each in our own different ways?"

"True." Molly sat quietly for a while, struggling

to capture the essence of Alaric. This was surely a chance to help his cause, and to do so honestly. And somehow, words seemed inadequate.

"I'm not a flowery speaker," she began, "so forgive me if I am plain."

"Plain is always preferable to flowery, I think."

"That's fortunate, then. If I had to choose one word to describe my king, I suppose I would have to say that he is *good*. But that's too plain, even for me. And if I had to choose a second word, it would be *complicated*.

"The path of Alaric's life was never of his own choosing. He was a third son, so it was assumed he'd never rule. Nor would he inherit much. He'd have to make his own way in the world, as younger sons of all great and noble houses must. And like them, he only had two choices: he could enter the priesthood and become a bishop, or be trained as a knight and go to war. He didn't want to do either one. So his parents sent him off to Austlind in hopes that his cousin Reynard could make a soldier out of a small, bookish boy who was none too fond of horses.

"I never saw him during that time, so I can't say how he behaved; but I can guess that it was hard for him—out there in the practice yard day after day, training with swords and lances along with Reynard's sons. Well, I'll let you imagine it. They are very unlike, those boys and Alaric. He would have felt like a bird trapped under the sea."

The princess smiled. "Yes," she said.

"Then, unexpectedly, he became king. I needn't tell you the circumstances, as you were there. He was only sixteen and had not been raised to carry such a burden of responsibility, nor did it come naturally to him. Yet I doubt there was ever a sovereign who tried more valiantly to learn than Alaric has and who put aside his personal hopes, and dreams, and desires more rigorously so he could focus his every thought on how best to govern his people."

"Edmund said much the same of him—that Alaric was true to his ideals."

"So he is. But it costs him, you know." Molly touched her hand to her heart.

The princess, seeing this, did the same. "I understand you," she said, "better perhaps than you might think. Alaric has lost his family. He has lost his freedom. And he has been given a task as difficult as it is important. And though he never wanted it, he has embraced it completely."

Molly's eyes narrowed as she studied the princess, who almost seemed to be talking about herself. "Yes," she said. "You have it exactly."

"But under all that devotion to duty, there's a little rebellious streak."

Molly's eyes widened now.

"It fights against that which is inevitable; it seeks a way around the wall that divides one part of himself from another. It yearns. It aches. But he keeps it packed away and only takes it out when he's alone—or rarely, *very* rarely, when he is with someone he trusts. Then he shuts it up again, because he must."

"Merciful God," Molly whispered. "You are the same."

The princess struggled to master her emotions, and Molly looked away, giving her the privacy to do it. But she couldn't resist adding one more thing.

"Perhaps, together, you might break down that wall and be the better for it."

Betta drew in a deep breath. "Well, Molly, you have answered my question quite to my satisfaction."

"Rather more than you wanted, I fear."

"On the contrary. It was very illuminating. Now, if you will bear with me just a little longer, we shall finish with the chessmen. We're almost done, I promise."

"Of course. Go ahead."

"These last two pieces in the back row are rooks— you can call them castles if that's easier to remember.

They're second in power after the queen. And that follows a certain logic, since a king's castle offers him great protection—more than a knight or a bishop could."

Molly lifted her little ivory tower and turned it thoughtfully in her hand. Was Betta alluding to the fact that Alaric had been drawn from the safety of his castle? If so, was that a threat or a warning? God's teeth, but this was a strange situation! One moment Molly was as trusting as a child, and the princess was her intimate friend—and the next thing she knew there came a flood of doubt. She looked at Leondas for guidance or reassurance, but he was comfortably asleep in the princess's lap. Perhaps that was as good an answer as she was going to get.

"And finally," Betta said, putting down her castle, "we have a whole row of little lumps that look like gravestones. They are your pawns. They can only move one square at a time, straight ahead—except on the first move, when they can move two. Think of them as foot soldiers, out there on the front lines, where they'll likely be struck down by the first volley of arrows. That's why you have so many."

"Because they're expendable."

"Yes. Chess is about the strategy of war, and it's meant to reflect the true conditions on an actual field of battle. But you know . . ." She paused for a moment, and whatever she was thinking about, it seemed to please her. "Just as in the real world, the pawns—the common folk—sometimes rise above their humble origins and go on to achieve greatness. Not often, but it happens. And so our little pawn, if he manages to survive that first onslaught of enemy fire—and is strong enough, and brave enough, or maybe just lucky enough to keep moving through the ranks of the opposing army till he reaches the very last row on the other side—can be promoted to any piece he chooses. Except king, of course."

"You mean a pawn could be promoted to queen?"

"Most certainly," she said. "That's what most players do—but only if their original queen has already been lost. For even in chess, a king may not have two wives." The princess was gazing squarely at Molly now. "As in real life," she added.

In the silence that followed, they could hear Leondas purr.

❦ 13 ❧

A Matter of Payment

PRINCE RUPERT HAD NOTHING to do that morning, and he was unbearably bored.

His father was in conference with his chief advisers, working out strategy for that afternoon's meeting with King Gonzalo. Even if they'd invited Rupert to join them—which they very pointedly had not—he wouldn't have wanted to listen to them blather on anyway. It was all just, "If we offer him this, then what if Alaric offered him that? But we don't want to seem too eager, so maybe . . ."

Boring.

There was supposed to be a hunt soon, which

was something to look forward to. But that was in the future. And right now he thought that if he stayed cooped up in that ridiculous guesthouse for one more minute, he would scream. So he told one of his father's knights that he was going for a walk and left.

The Cortovans were apparently very keen on gardens, parks, and whatnot. Each of the clusters of villas was surrounded by green space—as if they were in the middle of the woods or something. It was nice, he guessed, but kind of strange. The usual thing was to have a castle with a city around it, and the walls and everything—and then you'd have the park someplace else.

Rupert didn't care much about flowers one way or the other. There were a lot of them in Cortova too. But then, it was a summery country. Hot and all.

He emerged from the woodsy area that surrounded their villas and came upon another group of buildings. The houses were just like everything else in the summer palace: plain as mush on the outside, no carving or decoration or anything, and open to the weather in the middle. The only difference was that these were smaller.

He heard voices and followed the sound—but stealthily, as if he were stalking a deer, creeping in close for a good shot. What he saw once he'd rounded a corner were the dancers from the other night: the almost-naked ones from that foreign place with the peculiar name.

Only they weren't naked now. They had on long white robes, like something you'd sleep in on a cold night, and they had skullcaps on their heads. They were arguing with a small group of soldiers. Or at least *one* of the dancers was; he seemed to be their leader. The rest of them stood behind him with scowls on their faces.

Meanwhile, slaves were coming and going in the background, hauling these big leather trunks out of the houses—probably costumes and instruments— and carrying them away in the direction of the stables.

So the dancers were leaving. What were they arguing about?

Rupert decided that this was interesting. He found himself a place where he could sit in the shade and watch them without being seen.

They were shouting now—the head dancer and the head soldier, each in his own language. Rupert couldn't understand either one, but he could tell a lot just by watching their gestures.

"*Ochorestew!*" the dancer cried (or something like that), his left fist defiantly on his hip, his right hand outstretched, palm up. He was asking for something, but not as beggars do. This was a demand, not a plea.

The head soldier, arms crossed over his chest, shook his head and said, "No." Rupert actually understood that. *Yes* and *no* were among the very few Cortovan words he remembered from his lessons.

The dancer pointed defiantly in the direction of the royal compound. Then once again he held out his palm, only now he poked it with his finger with such force that you might think he hoped to drill for water there.

"*Gobbledypollywhatever,*" said the dancer. "*Shukku-nokku dogwater.*" The rest of the troupe grumbled in agreement. Then all of them pointed at their palms.

Rupert was pretty sure he had it now: they hadn't been paid!

At all? Not enough? A day late? The king had clearly promised them something, and now they were being sent away without it.

Again the same gestures: pointing to the king's palace, then to the dancers' palms.

"*Ortollini mooly novotomoto woostoni,*" said the soldier, indicating first the dancers, then Gonzalo's palace, and finally spreading his arms wide and gazing up into the sky, as if to take in the whole world: *Once you've performed for the king of Cortova, every noble in the land will want to hire you. You ought to be paying us for the privilege!*

The dancers, all uncommonly large and muscular men, now began to advance on the soldiers in a menacing manner. Eagerly, Rupert leaned forward. The dancers far outnumbered the soldiers. And though they probably hadn't been trained as knights, they had these little sickle-shaped swords hanging from their belts; and anyone who'd seen them dance would know how swift and powerful they were.

The head guard held up his hand: *Wait!* He did it two more times: *Wait, wait!* Then as if creeping away from a snarling dog, the soldiers left.

The head dancer watched them go with a mocking smile. But he didn't move—except to order the slaves to stop carrying out their goods. Then he and his fellow dancers waited, arms crossed, for a fairly long time—certainly long enough for Rupert to grow restless. But he forced himself to stay and keep watching, because he had the feeling that this little encounter was nowhere near over. And if there was going to be a sword fight, he didn't want to miss it.

So, he thought, *either the guards have gone back to get the money, or they are rounding up reinforcements.* Rupert would have bet on the latter. King Gonzalo was not the sort to be pushed around by a troupe of naked dancers.

Maybe he'd order his soldiers to chop off their

heads! *That* would be something to see!

All the same, it was an odd business, and there was a puzzle in it somewhere. Because everyone knew it was *really bad form* for a king—especially one who's so bloody rich—not to pay those who are "in his hand." It made him look . . . miserly. Small. *Poor.* His subjects would despise him. So why would Gonzalo humiliate himself, and get a bad reputation, all over a few gold coins? It made no sense—unless he wasn't as bloody rich as he wanted everyone to think.

No, surely not!

But then again, the princess hardly had any jewels. Both nights she'd dressed like a . . . like a lady-in-waiting or something. His father seemed to think she'd done it on purpose to show that she was so pretty she didn't *need* any ornament. But Rupert found that hard to believe. Ladies liked their frippery. It was a well-known fact.

So. What if they really *were* poor, except that they already had all those fancy things lying around—the gold and silver platters, and the candlesticks, and those antique glasses his father was so excited about—and they just brought them out to make themselves *look* rich.

That really was something to think about! Rupert tried very hard to do it.

What if Cortova *used* to be rich but then something happened, and now they weren't? Just suppose: What would King Gonzalo do? He'd need to get himself some more money, that's what. And how would he do that? Well, the usual way was to make war: take land and treasure from some other kingdom. But war was famously expensive. You might get away with cheating the entertainers, but you'd bloody well better pay your army. And also there were the horses and the wagons, the catapults and cannons—they cost money too.

So wouldn't it be easier to find two kings who hated each other and were afraid of each other, and who wanted to ally themselves with you—and bring them together at your summer palace and let them *compete*, like jousters in the lists? Let them fight it out to see who wins, with each one offering a better deal than the other till . . .

Bloody hell—could that be *it*?

The soldiers were coming back now. And as Rupert had predicted, they'd gone for reinforcements. Quite a lot of them, actually. A small army, in fact. And though the dancers trembled with outrage at the injustice, they saw that they were beaten and allowed themselves to be escorted—three knights to a man— out of the summer palace.

Rupert was disappointed that there hadn't been

any beheadings, but his mind was on bigger things now. Long after the dancers and soldiers had disappeared from sight and there was nothing to look at but slaves carrying baggage, Rupert stayed where he was, in his shady spot, thinking.

If his father had nothing to gain—that is, if King Gonzalo really had been leading them on, trying to trick one or the other of them into giving him piles of money in exchange for a worthless alliance—then what should they do? Go home, that's what! Let Alaric pay Cortova's debts.

But suppose Rupert was mistaken? If he was, then to leave Cortova would be a very, very bad idea. Because Alaric and Gonzalo would then form an alliance and combine their armies, and that would be the end of it for Austlind. The problem was, you couldn't be sure.

But wait, he thought. Hold on. Why were they in Cortova in the first place? To get an alliance . . . because King Alaric was building up his army, and that was a threat to Austlind; and if Alaric got the alliance first, their goose was cooked. Rupert covered his face with his hands, deep in concentration. His brain had never worked this hard before in all his life.

What if you took Gonzalo, and the whole question of whether Cortova was rich or poor, out of the story entirely? Gonzalo wasn't the problem—Alaric was!

Oh! This was good. He was almost there!

And since Alaric wasn't married and didn't have an heir, and since Rupert's father was next in line for the throne, why not just kill Alaric, blame it on Gonzalo, and go home to rule both kingdoms?

Rupert lay back on the grass, gripping his head in his hands. By all the saints in heaven, he was brilliant, absolutely brilliant! He couldn't wait to tell his father!

❦ 14 ❧

Three Kings,
Two Negotiations

Morning session,
King Alaric:

Gonzalo's council chamber was uncommonly small. The rulers of ancient Cortova did not hold great audiences with vast numbers of their subjects. They only needed a space appropriate for meeting with their generals to plan campaigns of conquest, or for discussing matters of state with important senators, or occasionally for negotiating terms with visiting monarchs—as Gonzalo was doing now.

At the far end of the chamber was a dais, in the center of which sat a handsome throne in the antique style. But Gonzalo had chosen not to use it today. Instead, he and Alaric sat companionably together in the middle of the room, their chairs set at the precise angle that allowed them to look at each other without being forced to stare face-to-face. Between them, on a small, round table, sat a bowl of fruit and two antique glasses filled with honey-colored wine.

Two kings, meeting as equals—that was the desired effect.

"I hope you enjoyed last night's dinner," Gonzalo began.

"Yes, it was quite astonishing." *In so many ways.*

"Good, good! We do our best under the circumstances."

"No great hall, you mean?" Alaric said with a wry smile.

"Yes. Alas."

He paused then, and Alaric expected Gonzalo to move on to the business at hand. But in this he was disappointed.

"So how goes it in Westria?" he asked. "Settling in nicely on your throne?"

"Yes," Alaric replied, quite aware that King Gonzalo knew exactly how things had been going in Westria: the unrest among his nobles, the plots, and the threat of war with his cousin. "Very nicely."

"Glad to hear it! Such a lot of responsibility for a young lad like yourself, and so sudden, too—why, you never even got to finish your training as a knight. Or do I misremember?"

Alaric smiled. "No, my lord Gonzalo. Your memory is perfect."

"What a shame."

"Indeed."

"Well!" Gonzalo said, leaning into the word for emphasis so it would be clear that he was changing the subject. "You and I have important business to discuss, do we not? And as I have an appointment with King Reynard this afternoon, our time is limited. But we can at least make a beginning. You know, get the old stone rolling down the hill? Then we can go chasing after it tomorrow. What do you say?"

Alaric nodded. Then, in case that wasn't clear enough, he said, "Yes, Gonzalo, let's get started."

"Won't you try one of the apricots? They're exceptionally sweet this year."

"No, thank you."

"Well, suit yourself." He settled back in his chair, gave a great, significant sigh, and began, as promised, to "make a beginning."

"If you don't mind," he said, "I think it would be best if I went first—just to make everything clear, you know. Put it out there where the cows can get at it, as the farmers like to say." He waited for Alaric to nod in agreement, then smiled in that now all-too-familiar way that generally preceded something unpleasant.

"You are aware, of course, that Cortova is blessed with an extensive coastline on the Southern Sea, and the wealth of my kingdom has always come from trade. That was true in the Golden Age of Emperors; but it's even more so now, as we have no ambitions to build an empire, as my ancestors did. We depend entirely on commerce.

"And so, for many years, going back to my great-great-grandfather's time, Cortova has chosen to remain neutral. I'm sure you can understand why. If we were to ally ourselves with, say, Gronnigstadt and you were at war with them, you would not want to do business with us—now would you?"

Alaric didn't like the direction this was tending, and he was more than a little tired of being toyed with. So he left Gonzalo's obvious question unanswered. He just sat in silence and waited for him to answer it himself.

"Of course you wouldn't! Worse still, I would be obliged to send troops and money to help Gronnigstadt defeat you—which would be of no conceivable advantage to Cortova. With this in mind, you can surely see that an alliance with Westria would be of no interest to me whatsoever."

Alaric started and caught his breath. . . .

Afternoon session,
King Reynard:

Reynard and Gonzalo sat together informally, like two old friends, cups of wine and a bowl of fruit ready at hand. The late-afternoon sun streamed in through the windows, turning the marble floors to gold.

"Did you enjoy our humble little dinner last night? I hope you and Rupert were pleased."

"It was splendid. Thank you."

"Food not too spicy?"

"Not at all."

"Excellent!"

A tantalizing moment of silence followed, then, "What a handsome lad your Rupert is—sturdy, you know. Manly."

"Yes, well, he's grown up among boys. Rough and tumble."

"You have *three* sons, I believe."

Reynard agreed that he did, quite aware that Gonzalo didn't *believe* he had three sons; he knew it for a positive fact, along with their names, their ages, the color of their eyes, and what they liked to have for breakfast. For some reason, Reynard found this ongoing pretense of ignorance particularly hard to bear.

"And all of them still at home," Gonzalo continued. "Unusual. You don't hold with the old thinking that boys learn better if they're sent away to some other noble house, where they can be trained up for knighthood without their mothers hovering over them and their nursemaids drying their tears?"

Reynard opened his mouth to respond but was too angry to find the words; and by the time he'd thought of a few, Gonzalo had moved on.

"I believe your cousin Alaric was fostered with you, was he not? Though of course he didn't finish his training—what with the tragedy and all, and his needing to step up and rule the kingdom in his brother's place." He stopped at this point, apparently feeling he had goaded Reynard quite enough. Now he smiled as if they'd just been discussing the weather and waited.

"I'm astonished that you should ask me that," Reynard said. "About my boys—considering that you have kept young Castor home as well."

"So I have, *so I have*! What a fine pair we are, you and I, such overfond parents. But then, one has to consider who would be the *right* person to take a boy in hand, you know, and train him up properly. And while some run-of-the-mill prince would probably do well wherever you put him, the heir to a great throne must be handled with special care."

Reynard said not a word. He just stared at his host, wondering what in blazes had been the point of all that. Was Gonzalo hoping that *he* might foster Prince Castor himself? Well, he certainly hoped not, because even on brief acquaintance, that child had struck him as right peculiar. . . .

Morning session, continued,
King Alaric:

"As for my daughter," Gonzalo said to the dumbstruck Alaric, "she was married to the prince of Slovarno when they were both just children and widowed shortly thereafter. Then, of course, she was betrothed to your brother. In neither case did I seek—or allow—any kind of treaty or alliance to be part of the marriage contract, just the usual financial arrangements.

"Both matches ended poorly. The young prince died of the pox before he even came of age, and then there was that dreadful business in Westria. Sorry to bring it up. I know it must be painful for you. But so it was for my daughter, too. And not surprisingly, after that she expressed the wish to remain a maiden all her life.

"So you see, Alaric, she doesn't really *want* to marry—you or anyone else."

King Gonzalo now folded his hands, smiled, fluttered his lashes, and shrugged.

"That's it?"

"In a nutshell, yes."

Afternoon session, continued,
King Reynard:

"She doesn't *want* to marry?"

"As I just said."

"And you cannot persuade her?"

"But that would be unkind, and I am such a *fond* parent—weren't we just discussing that?"

"And you have no interest in an alliance without a marriage?"

"None whatsoever."

"Then," Reynard said through clenched teeth, "may I ask why you allowed me—no, *demanded* that I travel all this way to discuss a marriage and an alliance that you now inform me you *do not want*? Is it 'in the interest of Cortova' to house, feed, and entertain two royal parties for a week? Or were you just feeling lonely and bored out here in the country and longing for a bit of amusement?"

"Ah," said Gonzalo, taking an apricot and nibbling at it thoughtfully, then making a show of wiping the juice from his beard with a linen napkin. "I believe we have reached the heart of it now."

"I believe we have reached the *end* of it, my lord king. I believe it's time for me to go."

"Oh, do sit down, Reynard! Don't be so hasty. And you really must try one of these apricots."

"I didn't come to Cortova for the bloody fruit!"

"No, you're right. You didn't. But won't you please sit down? Thank you!

"Now, your question is fair: Why did I allow you to come all this way for nothing? Because, you see, you were so very *eager*, Reynard, so *pressing*; and I wasn't quite sure how to interpret that."

"*How to interpret it?* I want a match for my son, and I hoped to ally myself with Cortova. What else could it possibly have meant?"

"Nonsense! A subtle man like you? It might have meant any number of things—a veiled threat, for example: join with me or I'll bring my army across your border and take what I want."

Reynard was stupefied. "You can't be serious!"

"Oh, but I am. And I just thought I could get a

better feel for the situation if we were to meet together in person."

"Bloody hell!"

"But also . . ."

Morning session, continued,
King Alaric:

"Oh come, my dear Alaric—don't look at me like that!"

"How am I supposed to look? We've been discussing this matter since last winter, messengers running back and forth. And now you've put me to a great deal of trouble and expense by insisting that I come here in person to discuss the terms of the alliance and the marriage contract. Not to mention the fact that you've been secretly corresponding with my cousin at the same time so as to pit us against each other—which was not gentlemanly, Gonzalo, not at all. And now, to top it all, you claim no interest in either a marriage or an alliance? What was that all about?"

"Now, now, don't be angry, young Alaric. Your question is fair: Why *did* I allow you to come all this way for nothing? Because, you see, you were so very *eager*, so *pressing*; and I wasn't quite sure how to interpret that."

Afternoon session, continued,
King Reynard:

The king of Austlind was on his feet again. His face was flushed with anger, and he was breathing hard. "Also *what*, Gonzalo?"

"Also, I began to wonder whether—seeing as you were, as I said, *so eager* and *so pressing*—you might perhaps be willing to *make* it worth my while, and in my interest, to change the way I have heretofore looked upon the subject of alliances. In which case I might—the incentive being great enough—convince my daughter (whom you will surely have noticed is exceedingly beautiful and charming and quite strong enough to bear any number of little princes without giving you the trouble of dying in the process) to marry your son."

Morning session, continued,
King Alaric:

"And though my daughter's betrothal to your brother ended quite tragically and was most unsettling to the delicate feelings of a young girl, she is also an obedient daughter, and she will do her duty . . . if, of course, you make it worth my while. To my advantage, you see."

"You're a bloody wonder—you know that, Gonzalo?

Were you nursed in your cradle by a viper?"

"Come now, young Alaric! There's no need to get personal about it."

"Of course not. This is just business."

"*Exactly!* I'm so glad you understand."

❦ 15 ❧

An Impossible Decision

MOLLY SAT ON A bench under a tree, waiting for Alaric to come back. She could have waited for him in his villa, but that would have meant braving Lord Brochton. Besides, it was quiet and peaceful in the dappled shade of the garden.

She heard him before she saw him, his quick, heavy footfalls as expressive as the thunder on his face. When he saw Molly, he sent his escort away and joined her on the bench without a word.

"That bad?" she asked.

"Worse."

"He's chosen Reynard already?"

"No. It seems Gonzalo doesn't actually want an alliance—never has wanted one; it would be bad for business."

"What? Then why would he drag you—"

"As for the princess, she's not inclined to marry, me or anybody else."

"But—"

"By the saints, will you *stop interrupting*?"

Molly shut her mouth.

"This was just the opening gambit, you see. It seems he *might* bring himself to rethink the alliance, and he *might* be able to persuade the princess to do her duty—if I'm willing to make it *worth his while.*"

She waited until she was absolutely sure that Alaric had finished speaking. Then, "Just adding some more kindling to the fire? First Reynard pops up unexpected and unwelcome. Now he's playing the reluctant maiden."

"It was insufferable. I almost strangled him."

"It's well that you didn't."

"I'm not so sure."

"Do you think he'll say the same things to Reynard this afternoon?"

"Undoubtedly. Maybe Reynard will strangle

Gonzalo for me. He's always had a hot temper."

"Alaric," she said softly, "do you still want the alliance?"

"Not really. Not at all. But if I leave Cortova, Reynard will get it for himself—and on more advantageous terms. I can't let that happen."

"Do you still want the princess?"

"I have nothing against the princess, except that Gonzalo is her father."

"You've told me countless times that you must marry soon and get yourself an heir."

"It's still true."

"Then, Alaric, it's time you gave her the cup. It's the only advantage you have over Reynard. And if she's truly reluctant to marry—though I don't believe she is; I think that was just Gonzalo playing you along—a sip from the cup will change her mind and make sure she chooses you and not Prince Rupert."

"I doubt she'll get to choose. She's nothing but a pawn in Gonzalo's little game. And if Reynard wins, then like it or not she'll marry Prince Rupert. And if I've already given her the cup, she'll spend the rest of her life pining for me and I for her. I don't dare risk it."

"Everything you say is true and well thought out—except for one. Whatever else Elizabetta may be, she is *not* anyone's pawn."

"What do you mean?"

"She *is* Gonzalo's daughter, as you pointed out. She's strong and smart, determined and perceptive. And she has a will of iron. That girl won't 'be persuaded' to do anything that goes against her nature. If you give her the cup and she drinks from it, she's yours. And if it comes to a contest between father and daughter, I'd put my money on the princess any day."

He gazed down at his boots for a long time, thinking. Finally, without looking up, he said, "Poor Molly. I put you to so much trouble getting that cup."

"Oh, for heaven's sake, that has nothing to do with it. I wouldn't care if you threw the blasted thing off a cliff. I just want you to get what you came for. If you can see another way to secure the kingdom, then let's pack up right now and get out of here."

"Unfortunately, I can't. You have to hand it to Gonzalo: he made sure that neither of us can afford to leave."

"Then what?"

"I'll give her the cup."

"Tonight, at dinner?"

"No, not with Reynard looking on."

"Tomorrow then?"

"As soon as I can arrange a private audience."

"I'm sorry, Alaric, but better now than later. This

bidding war, it might get out of hand; and it would be well to have Betta in your camp right from the beginning."

"Betta?" He raised his brows in mock amazement. "You're calling her 'Betta' now?"

"She asked me to."

"Be careful, Molly."

"I'm trying. She's very seductive."

"I know. All the more reason."

They sat in silence, thinking. Alaric leaned down and picked up a stone and threw it into the bushes.

"So, now what?" she said. "Do you meet with Gonzalo again tomorrow?"

He barked out a derisive laugh. "Oh, yes. We've hardly even begun. There's been no mention of terms at all, though I can already guess that the princess will have no dowry—quite possibly *I* shall be expected to pay for the privilege of having her to wife. Gonzalo will propose an alliance in which Westria has many obligations while Cortova has few, and a river of gold will flow south, toward Gonzalo. Naturally, I will point out how very unreasonable that is, and he will point out that my cousin Reynard might be a bit more willing, so perhaps I ought to think about it a little more carefully. And it will go on like that until one of us has either strangled the monster or has agreed to give him everything he wants."

"It sounds unbearable."

"It is. Now you must forgive me, Molly. I have to go inside and use the bathing pool—to wash Gonzalo's stink off my body. Then I may be sick. After that I'm not sure what I'll do."

Just as he'd arrived without a greeting, he left with no good-bye. And long after the door had closed behind him, she continued to sit on the bench, in the shade of an ancient olive tree, absorbing the enormity of what they'd just decided.

16

The Knight

LORD MARCUS HAD SEEN the princess many times over the years. He'd watched her grow from a pretty child into a beautiful woman. But it had always been from a distance, on formal court occasions, so in truth he didn't really know her at all. Then he'd been chosen to command the guard that would escort her to Westria for her marriage to King Edmund.

He hadn't expected to like her. As a princess and a famous beauty, she was bound to be shallow and vain, with few subjects of conversation beyond fashion, parties, and gossip. She would, in short, be a bore.

Instead, she'd proved to be surprisingly bright.

And though her knowledge of the world was limited, she'd been quick and eager to learn, peppering Marcus with questions ranging from politics and history to poetry, science, and art. He'd found this charming, even a little touching, that she should be so willing to step out of the narrow confines of her privileged life and explore things that were difficult and new. He'd answered her questions as well as he could without flattery or condescension. And she'd been astonishingly grateful, hanging on his every word as if he were her superior and not the other way round.

That had been the beginning of their friendship.

Then one day it came up in conversation that Marcus played chess and that he never traveled anywhere without a board. Her lovely face had lit up with pleasure. Chess, she'd declared, was her greatest passion.

He'd smiled at this remark, instantly making all sorts of erroneous assumptions, most especially that by "passion" she meant that she liked to play now and then with her court ladies and that she found it to be jolly fun. Marcus, on the other hand, took the game quite seriously. So he'd cringed when she suggested they match their wits over a board that very afternoon.

But of course, there was no refusing. So he'd proceeded with caution, holding back and giving her the occasional opening to take a piece he'd never have lost if he'd been playing in earnest. He had sense enough not to lose on purpose: she'd figure it out and be insulted. But nor did he want to crush her with a quick defeat. So they'd plodded along for a while like a pair of beginners.

Then, on impulse, he'd made a move—he hadn't been able to stop himself; it was just so clever—and she'd looked up at him with those amazing eyes, a flash of understanding crossing her face. Then she'd stared at the board for a spell, all fierce concentration, and countered with an even better move (how had he missed it?). Suddenly they both broke into laughter, each recognizing the other as a worthy opponent. After that, and for the rest of the journey north, they'd gone at it hammer and tongs—may the best man (or woman) win. Their friendship had shifted again, growing deeper.

At last they'd arrived at Westria, where Elizabetta would live out the days of her life as the queen of King Edmund the Fair. And Marcus would return to Cortova and his service to King Gonzalo. Or at least that's what they'd expected. Instead, there'd been the banquet, and the wolves.

Marcus had rescued the princess that night, carrying her out through the fleeing throng to safety. She'd been so covered with gore he'd feared for her life. But neither fang nor claw had touched her. The blood had all been Edmund's.

That didn't mean she hadn't been wounded. Quite the contrary, she'd been so damaged by what she'd witnessed that for a time she'd all but lost her mind. And it fell to Marcus to help her recover.

Unfortunately, his training as a knight had not prepared him for such a task. He could strike down an enemy soldier at a full gallop, but he didn't know how to mend a broken spirit. All he could think to do was to assure her that she was safe now, to treat her with gentle kindness, and to get her back to Cortova as quickly as possible.

For the first two weeks of their return journey, she'd refused to leave his side. She wouldn't even ride her own horse but insisted on sitting with him. He found this awkward and rather too intimate: sharing a saddle with the princess, who rested between his arms, her head turned back so she could lean against his breast. Even at night he had to sit at her bedside, ready to reach out and take her hand when she woke from her nightmares screaming.

Be assured, they were never alone in her chamber. That would have been scandalously improper. They were always chaperoned by a group of court ladies. He'd had a dark little chuckle with himself about that—for even if he *had* been the sort of man who went about ravishing maidens, he'd have been far too exhausted to do it.

Then, near the end of the second week, the princess had started to recover. By the time they'd crossed the border, she'd become more or less herself. Marcus understood that she was still healing—she might well go on healing for years—but she rode beside him on her own mount now, and the night terrors had mostly stopped.

"Marcus," she'd said one day, "when we get back to Pelenos, you mustn't tell anyone how I behaved."

"I would never speak of your private affairs to anyone, my lady—though there's nothing to be ashamed of. What happened that night was dreadful. It would have disturbed anyone to witness such a massacre, and so close at hand."

"Well, I *am* ashamed. I was pitiful and weak. I made a fool of myself, and I don't want anyone to know. Please tell the others—your knights, and my ladies, and the servants—that they mustn't say a word. Swear them to silence, Marcus. Make it an order. Look very stern."

"Like this?" He'd made a ferocious face.

And for the first time since they'd left Dethemere Castle, the princess had laughed.

⁂

They'd said good-bye in the entry court of the great Lion Hall. He'd bowed, she'd whispered her thanks, and they'd gone their separate ways. He'd assumed that, once again, he'd see her only at a distance, on public occasions. And that had felt strange to him after all they'd shared those past weeks, being together every moment of every one of those days. He'd tried very hard to convince himself that it would be a relief. He'd done his duty and done it well. Now he was a free man.

But he hadn't felt relieved; he'd felt hollow. Caring for her, keeping her safe, and helping her to heal had been the most challenging and meaningful tasks of his life. They had filled him with purpose, and he missed it.

Then, not a week later, a note had arrived, inviting him to her chambers for a game of chess. When Marcus read it, he'd blushed like a lad of thirteen. Even now, a year and a half later, he dared not admit to himself how much he looked forward to their games, which had become a regular thing, once or twice a week.

They still played hard, and the princess still asked questions. Indeed, at times she seemed to be less interested in the game than in what she could learn from him.

Gonzalo was not one of those enlightened kings who believed in educating daughters. A princess only needed to master the lady-arts: sewing, dancing, music, and whatnot. It was useful to speak a couple of languages and to write an elegant hand; and if she wanted to amuse herself by reading a bit of poetry, there was probably no harm in that. But Elizabetta's sole purpose, like that of any princess, was to be married off to the advantage of her kingdom. So there was absolutely no call to bother herself with things such as politics, history, statecraft, or war.

These were, of course, the very subjects she most wished to learn about. So as they played, Marcus explained the various alliances and conflicts on the continent. He laid out the pedigrees of certain kings, describing their characters and family connections. He told her the long, colorful saga of Cortova's rich history, from the splendors of its ancient past, through its sad decline, to its present return to wealth and power as a great merchant kingdom. He threw in a bit of geography and some musings on diplomacy and regaled her with a few war stories.

Marcus had become her window on the world.

⚜

Now, on this particular afternoon, he arrived to find her in the atrium as usual. The chessboard was ready, and the slaves had set out a tray of fruit and dainties for them to enjoy while they played.

"I'm surprised you have time for a game," he said, "with your suitors here and another formal dinner tonight."

Marcus knew little of women, but he'd always assumed that getting dressed was a lengthy and involved process: the arranging of hair, the choosing of clothes, the jewels, the perfume, the plucking and painting. He could only imagine.

"Oh," she said, "it won't take very long. I'm going as myself these days. It's so much quicker."

He noted her hair, which hung straight down her back, still wet from washing, and the faded blue tunic she wore, soft with age and damp around the shoulders.

"I *will* change my clothes," she said with a chuckle. "And my hair should be dry by then. Oh, don't just stand there, Marcus; have a seat. White must begin."

She seemed unusually merry that day. He wondered if she had some great announcement to make, some surprise she was about to spring. But all she seemed to have was a new move, which took him off guard and cost him a bishop, and a lot more questions.

"I've been thinking," she said, "about alliances."

"Oh?" he replied.

"Yes. Father never wanted one before. He's always insisted Cortova must remain neutral."

He nodded. "That has traditionally been the way of things."

"Then why do you suppose he wants one now—enough to make such a production out of it, with the rival suitors and all?"

He took one of her pawns, but he did it mechanically. His mind was no longer on chess.

"Do we *need* an alliance, Marcus? Is there some problem I don't know about?"

"Your move, my lady."

"Answer me first."

He ran his tongue over his teeth and stared silently down at the board.

"I'm part of the bargain, you know," she said. "My marriage will seal the alliance. Now, I really don't want to marry that unpleasant little brat from Austlind. The very thought is repellant to me. And I certainly don't want to marry Edmund's brother, and go back to Westria, and dine every night in the same hall where . . . well, you understand. So do me a kindness, Marcus. Tell me why I must choose the one or the other. I'll go to my unwanted wedding with a lighter heart if I know it's truly important to Cortova."

He nodded, considering that *he* also had duties, and chief among them was keeping the king's secrets. All the same, she was King Gonzalo's daughter, not just any old person. And her point had struck home: she really did have a right to know why she was being auctioned off, especially after what she'd suffered already.

"My dear lady," he said at last, "you asked me once to keep a secret. I promised I would and so I have. Now I must ask you to do the same. What I am about to tell you, you must never repeat. Even after it becomes widely known, as no doubt it will, you must never say you heard it first from me." He kept his voice low, so the slaves wouldn't hear.

"I give you my oath."

He took a deep breath, then leaned even closer and spoke in a whisper.

"In any negotiation," he began, "the party with the greatest need is in the weakest position. As it happens, our need is extreme, so that must remain a secret. But there are other reasons for secrecy, even more critical to Cortova than the terms of an alliance.

"Trade is the source of our wealth. Ships come and go from our ports every day, carrying goods to and from the many kingdoms that rim the Southern Sea. Are you familiar with the famous saying about the emperor's wife—that she must always be above suspicion? Well, the ships of a merchant kingdom must be above suspicion too. There can be no doubt that the valuable cargo they carry will arrive safely at its destination."

"I understand."

"Over these past two years, the Frasians have begun to challenge our supremacy. This took us very much by surprise. Frasia was never strong enough to challenge anyone before, let alone a kingdom like Cortova. But it seems they've recently acquired a fleet of fast, new warships. They hunt in packs, seizing our merchant vessels, murdering the crews, and taking possession of the cargos.

"*That's* Cortova's terrible secret, my lady, the thing the world must not know."

They locked eyes. Elizabetta nodded. "The world will not learn it from me."

"We've been blaming the lost ships on pirates and have reimbursed the clients in full for the value of their goods, assuring them that we're taking extra measures now to keep the trade routes safe and are dealing with the pirates severely, as they deserve."

"How did Frasia get to be so strong and bold all of a sudden?"

"Our spies inform us that a certain rich and powerful king has ambitions to take control of the Southern Sea. But his country is landlocked, so he's formed an alliance with Frasia—which may be poor and badly ruled but has an extensive coastline and several excellent deepwater ports. So this powerful king has been sending Frasia vast quantities of gold to finance the building of ships, as well as the troops to man them."

"And this powerful king?"

"It doesn't matter, my lady—though if you were to go to your father's library and look closely at a map, I imagine you'd figure it out. All you really need to know is that Cortova will soon be at war, and everything depends upon the outcome. To win, we'll need to double, or even triple, our fleet. But building ships is costly, and our money comes from trade, which means we'll need even more warships to protect our merchantmen.

"Your father has the shipyards at Loras and Bottano working day and night. I would imagine that by now the treasury is . . ." He searched for the right word. He didn't want to say *depleted* or *exhausted*. ". . . reduced," he finally said.

They were silent for a long time.

"Thank you," she said at last. "I know that was hard and went against your conscience."

"You deserved to know."

"Yes. You did the right thing. And someday, Marcus, I promise you will understand why."

Part Three

Middlegame—the phase between the opening and the endgame, after development has been completed by both sides.

Day Four

❦ 17 ❧

Sigrid

THAT NIGHT MOLLY DREAMED of the cat again. "The game of chess is like the game of war," he said.

This time Leondas wasn't in the princess's garden. He was perched on a marble railing that ran along a terrace overlooking the sea. Beyond this railing was a narrow strip of grass that ended abruptly at the edge of a cliff. In her vision, Molly could hear the crash of waves on the rocks far below.

"I already know that," she said.

"In chess, as in war, there can be no victory without sacrifice."

Molly was sitting up now, fully awake. She hadn't

much liked this last remark.

"What *are* you anyway?" she asked, since that seemed to be the essential question. Talking animals had never appeared in her visions before.

"I am a cat."

"No, you're not. Cats don't speak. You may have taken the form of a cat, but you're really something else. I want to know what."

"Maybe you should ask Sigrid. She's wise; she might give you an answer. And you haven't talked with her in a very long time."

Molly blinked. "How could you possibly know about Sigrid? I've only told Alaric about her, and I doubt you learned it from him."

"*You* know about Sigrid."

"Well, of course I do. You're not making sense."

"Yes, I am. You just have to think about it."

"Look, if you're trying to help me, then please stop talking in riddles, because—"

But the cat was already leaving. He'd jumped off the railing onto the grass. Now he sauntered away in the disdainful manner of cats the world over.

"Thanks," she muttered.

Then more loudly, "Thank you *so very much*!"

Molly's attendant, Esther, who slept on a bench outside the chamber, had apparently heard Molly scolding the cat. Now she opened the door a crack and whispered, "My lady, are you all right?"

"I'm fine. It was just a dream. I think I'll get up and walk around a bit, clear it out of my head."

"Is there anything I can do?"

"No, thank you, Esther. Go back to sleep."

Molly made her way to the far end of the villa, where the bathing room was. She went inside and shut the door gently so as not to wake the others.

The room was steamy and smelled of sulfur from the hot springs that fed the pool. Moving carefully in the darkness, she removed her sleeping tunic, unbraided her hair, and slipped into the water. She gasped with pleasure as the warmth embraced her, and she stood there for a long time, her arms outstretched, floating. Then she bent her knees and squatted down till she was entirely underwater. Her hair fanned out around her face like a mermaid's. She felt her body go slack, the tension melting away. She went up for air, then dropped down again, into this other world where she was weightless and everything was warm.

After a long while Molly climbed out and lay on the deck, wrapped in a linen towel. The clay tiles beneath her were heated by the pipes that carried the water to the pool. The still, humid air caressed her. The world outside still lingered in the hush of early morning.

She could focus now. And as the cat had pointed out, it had been far too long since she'd spoken with Sigrid.

⚡

Sigrid was one of the twelve counselors of Harrows-gode (there were thirteen, if you counted the Chief Counselor, Soren Visenson, whose title was Great Seer). And since the council members were chosen from the wisest Magi with the greatest Gifts, there could be no doubt that Sigrid was an exceptional person. Yet Molly had found her repellant at first. And she was not alone in this.

For Sigrid's great, pale slab of a face, verging on ugly to begin with, seemed incapable of smiling or indeed wearing any expression but boredom and disdain. And when she spoke, her words were as cutting as her voice was cold. But it was the fierce directness of her gaze that made people shudder and turn away. It gave the unsettling impression that she knew exactly what they were thinking.

This, of course, was only an illusion—except in one particular case. She actually *could* read Molly's thoughts. Worse still, Molly could read hers. She knew, for example, that Sigrid thought she had the brains of a goat.

The discovery of this strange connection had surprised and unsettled them both, and each had scrambled to build mental walls to keep out the other. Only later did they realize that their Gifts had been linked for a purpose, because they were meant to help each other.

This had happened on the day Molly left Harrowsgode. She and her companions had made it up the switchback trail and were about to enter the narrow canyon that cut through the mountains. Suddenly they'd noticed that the lofty clouds of late afternoon had unaccountably turned dark. And then they'd heard the growl of thunder.

Molly had understood at once that this was not the work of nature. The weather in Harrowsgode had long been controlled by magic, and it never rained during the harvest. No, these storm clouds had been summoned by the Great Seer to keep Molly from leaving. For once it started raining, the canyon would become a raging river, and everyone in it would drown.

Molly and her companions had decided to chance it anyway, and Soren had hit them with everything he had.

Sigrid had saved them that day, not by challenging Soren—her Gift was not equal to his—but by scolding Molly for losing heart.

If you are the great Magus I think you are, came

Sigrid's voice in her head, *then you can find your powers even now. . . . But, Molly dear, you will at least have to try!*

The situation had been completely hopeless. Giving up was the only sensible thing to do. But because Sigrid had challenged her, Molly decided to fight. She'd harnessed her Gift in a way she hadn't done before—and the result had been past all imagining. Not only had she saved herself and her companions, she'd freed Harrowsgode from the grip of Soren's heavy hand.

Because you defeated him by feat of combat, Sigrid had explained, *he has lost his position as Great Seer. And because he used his sacred powers with the intention of taking lives, he will be banished from the Magi altogether.*

That had been quite amazing, and there was more to come. For by challenging Soren and overpowering him, Molly had become Great Seer in his place.

So she never truly left her ancestral home. Through Sigrid she could still be a part of it, no matter where she went. She could act as the council's eyes and ears, teaching them about the world beyond their walls. And together with the others, she could help her people return to the ways of old King Magnus: upholding the sanctity of life, foreswearing war and weapons, and always, always embracing the love of learning.

Since then Molly and Sigrid had wandered in and out of each other's minds with the trust and ease of two old friends who've shared a house for years. And now as Molly lay in the warm darkness, she followed the cat's advice.

᷄ ᷅

Sigrid? She didn't speak the name, just formed it silently in her mind.

Sigrid?

Sigrid!

I'm here, Molly. I was asleep.

Sorry. I've been up for a while, and I forgot it wasn't morning yet.

That's all right. It's a good time, really—no distractions. I've been listening these past weeks, and I know what's going on. But now I really think we need to talk.

That's what the cat said.

The one with the probing questions and the interesting facts about chess?

Yes. I asked him what the devil he was, and he seemed to think you'd know.

Well, I'm flattered by his confidence, but all I can do is guess. There's frequent mention in the literature of sorcery and magic of so-called "familiars": spirit guides that take animal form.

Well, if that's what he is, then he's not very good at it—guiding, I mean.

I'm not sure that's fair. He's clearly linked to you, as I am. He knows what you know but also things you don't, and he tells you about them. The chess talk, I'll admit, is a puzzle. But he got you to rethink Gonzalo's invitation, which led you to be wary of Reynard. He's attached himself to the princess, which probably means that you can trust her. And he suggested that you reach out to me—which was certainly wise.

I'm sorry it's been so long, Sigrid. First I was sick. Then I got here and things—

I know how things are.

Then you'll understand that until this is over, I won't be much use to Harrowsgode.

On the contrary. Great matters are being decided in Cortova right now. The outcome could very well shift the balance of power all over the continent, and that affects us. Through you, it's as though little Harrowsgode actually has a seat at the table.

I don't have a seat at the table, Sigrid. I'm not involved in the negotiations.

Really? I thought I heard Alaric asking your advice. I believe I heard you giving it.

Well, yes. As to whether my advice was wise or not . . .

You seemed quite certain.

It's one of my failings. I'm so very sure of something—and the next thing you know, I'm having doubts. He's giving the cup to the princess this afternoon.

It's all arranged, then—the private meeting?

Yes. Gonzalo was predictably eager to receive his gifts.

And you feel absolutely wretched about it.

Of course I do. If Reynard wins the princess—

Yes, yes, I know. But it was Alaric's decision to make, not yours. It's his heart and his kingdom that are at stake, and he's perfectly aware of the risks. You just need to concentrate on keeping him safe.

I would if I knew how. But my Gift has gone all peculiar, just when I need it most. In the past it gave me warnings and showed me the things I needed to know. Now it gives me nothing—just this terrible foreboding of tragedy and a cat who talks about chess. Besides urging Alaric to be careful, which I've done a thousand times—not that he listens to me—what more can I do?

Sigrid?

Sigrid?

I was thinking, dear.

Oh.

It's often a useful thing to do. Now listen, Molly. Your Gift is changing. Whenever that happens, it's generally for a reason. Let's try to figure out what that reason is. I would like to start by asking you some questions.

All right.

You told me about that night in Westria when you and Tobias saved Alaric's life. What did you see in the visions that led up to it?

Well, first there were people plotting to murder the royal family, though I didn't know who they were till later. Then on the night of the banquet I saw the wolves coming into the hall.

Did you see King Edmund die? In your vision?

Oh, yes. It was horrible.

Anything to do with Alaric?

No.

So everything you saw turned out to be true. There was a plot. The wolves came. And they killed King Edmund.

What are you saying?

Molly, I believe that in this life—even for you, great as you are—there are matters of fate that are written in the stars. They cannot be changed. Edmund's death was one of them.

Then why did my spirit bother sending me all those warnings?

Obviously, that's the question, dear. Why don't we think it through?

You were warned that King Edmund would die, but his fate was already sealed, so you never had the power to save him. But Alaric's fate was not yet written. And because you knew about the plot and the curses, because you'd seen how Edmund would die, you acted differently that night than you might otherwise have done. When the wolves arrived, you understood they weren't real but rather a manifestation of a curse sent to destroy the royal family. And therefore you knew that when they'd finished their grizzly business in the hall, they'd go looking for Alaric next. That's why you and Tobias ran back up those stairs, and that's why you were able to save him.

That makes sense, but it doesn't answer the question. If it worked so well before, why is it changing now? Why does my spirit give me nothing but dread? It's like I'm grieving, but I don't know who I'm grieving for. It's just wearing me down and it isn't useful at all.

I suspect your spirit is protecting you in some way. Since it's never let you down before, perhaps you'll just have to trust that it will tell you what you need to know when you need to know it.

I wish it'd just get it over with and tell me now.

And I wish you had a little more patience.

It's hard.

Yes. And I'm afraid it's going to get harder. You'd better be ready.

What do you mean? Sigrid, sometimes you're as mysterious as that bloody cat.

Molly, remember the day you left Harrowsgode? You were

in the canyon in a flood. A surge of water had washed you out of your saddle; and you were holding on with one hand as you were carried down that rushing river, being slammed against the canyon walls by the sheer force of it, the dark waters tugging at your skirts, trying to pull you down.

Of course I remember.

You were already half drowned, and the roar of the flood was in your ears, and there was no way you could possibly survive. Yet you didn't give up; you fought back. You closed your mind to everything that was going on around you and reached down and took control of your powers. And you did it with such fierce determination that you turned nature on its head. You caused the water to rise up and return to the clouds—every drop, so that even your clothes were dry. And then you cleared the sky.

Why are you telling me what I already know?

Just a reminder, dear, of what you can do.

Because?

You might need to do something like that again, perhaps very soon.

❦ 18 ❧

The Loving Cup

ALARIC SAT ALONE IN his chamber. His audience with the royal family had been set for that afternoon, and he felt that what he was about to do deserved a few more minutes of quiet reflection.

He got up, opened the large wooden chest in the corner, and took out a handsome ebony box. He set this on his writing table, then went back to the chest for another, larger package: a round leather case lined with plum-colored velvet that pulled together at the top like a drawstring bag.

Alaric sat down again, the leather case in his lap; but he didn't open it right away. He just waited for a while, as though gathering his courage. Finally, he released the bow and pulled the velvet bag open to reveal an exquisite antique silver bowl.

Many years before, it had been a gift from the king of Austlind to the king of Westria on the occasion of the longed-for birth of a son and heir. The bowl was famous, one of Westria's great treasures, and had been proudly displayed at court on countless high occasions over the course of three generations.

Now, once again, it would serve as a gift from one royal house to another. And Gonzalo, being a man of refined tastes, would appreciate it for what it was: a masterpiece, an heirloom, and a priceless work of art. He would also know that it had originally been given by Reynard's parents in honor of Alaric's father. And now Alaric had quite publicly given it away.

Reynard was sure to be offended by this. And since Gonzalo was already stirring up antipathy between the two cousins, the bowl would be just one more weapon to use in his nasty little campaign. He'd bring it out before every dinner, forcing Reynard to wash his hands over it. And if somehow Reynard failed to recognize the thing, Gonzalo would call it to his attention. "See here, Reynard," he'd say, "look at this a handsome piece of silver young Alaric gave to me. Now, isn't it a wonder?"

None of this had been planned, of course. Alaric couldn't have known that Reynard would be there. He'd decided to give the bowl to Gonzalo because it was lavish and sure to please, it would save him the expense of buying something new, and most of all because he wanted the hateful thing out of his sight. Even now he couldn't bring himself to touch it. For this bowl, the great silver handbasin of Westria, had caused the death Alaric's entire family.

His grandfather, old King Mortimer, had been the first to die; he'd been snake-bit in wintertime, when serpents lie dormant in burrows and caves and never bite anyone. Much later, Alaric's father, King Godfrey the Lame, had been gored by a monstrous creature, a thing of such hideous deformity as was never seen before by human eyes. Then Prince Matthias, Alaric's oldest brother and the heir to the throne, had been strangled by a vine while hunting; it had appeared out of nowhere, dropping down like a hangman's noose as he rode by. And finally, on that terrible night just eighteen months past, a pack of demon wolves had entered the great hall of Dethemere Castle to finish off the rest: Alaric's mother; his sister, Elinor; and his brother, King Edmund the Fair.

Then the wolves had gone in search of Alaric and had found him on the stairs, quite unaware of what was happening below. Had it not been for Molly and Tobias, he'd have died along with the others, and the royal line of Westria would have come to an end.

This was such a spectacular, heartbreaking tale of woe—with its royal setting and many gruesome details—that people talked of it everywhere, the general opinion being that the House of Westria had been cursed by evil magic. This was true. But only a very few knew who had laid that curse and why.

Reynard, as it happened, was one of them.

He'd heard it first from Alaric and had laughed it off. Then he'd heard it from his mother, and this time he'd believed. Because she was the one who'd commissioned the great handbasin, then forced the silversmith to fill it with a hundred curses. She'd admitted this to his face.

Reynard had seen for himself what those curses could do that night in King Edmund's hall. And he would have noted—well, everyone had once they'd left off screaming and running for their lives—how precisely they'd gone about their slaughter, harming no one but the royal family of Westria.

And therein lay another wonderful stroke of blind luck. For when Gonzalo brought out the silver bowl, it would do more than just offend Reynard. It would serve as a reminder that if he were to take Alaric's throne—whether by murder or through force of arms—*he*, Reynard, would become the head of the House of Westria, and those very particular curses would then come after him—and his wife and his sons.

At least that's what Reynard would believe, since he didn't know that Molly (as usual, with the help of Tobias) had destroyed the last of the curses, so the bowl was completely harmless now. Alaric smiled as he pulled the drawstring closed and set the leather case aside. Now he took up the ebony box.

He removed the lid and peeled off the many layers of silk that protected the Loving Cup. He hefted the weight of it in his hands, turning it to admire its elaborate base. With its filigree and bright beading, ornaments raised and incised, and the many delicate enamels, dark against gleaming gold, it was an astonishing work of the silversmith's art. In contrast to the base and stem, the bowl of the cup was perfect simplicity: beaten silver on the outside, plated with gold on the inside. It caught the light streaming in through the windows and glowed like the very sun.

Just holding it, Alaric could feel its latent power—pulsing, eager, impatient to work out its purpose: to unite two people in a perfect love that would last as long as they lived and would thereafter bless their children, and their children's children, for generations to come.

"It's very powerful, Alaric," Molly had warned when she'd given him the cup. "The bond it forms can never be broken." (As if he hadn't already known that he was playing with fire!) When she'd added that he should use it wisely, he'd snapped at her.

"That has always been my intention."

"Good," she'd replied, locking eyes with him so fiercely that he hadn't been able to look away. "Because once the princess sets her lips to the cup, there's no turning back."

But Alaric's decision was firm now—formed over the course of a year and more by the careful weighing of help against harm, his duty as king against his private wishes, the greater good against the lesser need. Now nothing remained that he hadn't yet considered. It was never going to get any easier. He could stop thinking now.

❧ ❦

The chairs where Gonzalo and Alaric had sat together that morning, and where he'd likewise sat with Reynard that afternoon—grinding them down with his ever-escalating, outrageous demands, dropping the occasional wounding insult disguised as pleasant conversation—had been cleared away, along with the table, the bowl of fruit, and the glasses of chilled white wine. Now the room was empty, as a reception hall should be; and the king was seated on his throne, the prince and princess on either side of him. All three were wearing crowns.

"We welcome you, my lord king of Westria," Gonzalo said, adopting the formal manner common on such occasions.

"I thank you for receiving me," Alaric replied with a slight bow such as one ruler gives to another.

He'd brought with him six of his knights. One carried the bowl in its round leather case, another the ebony box, and a third had a falcon perched on his fist, which was sheathed in a sturdy leather glove.

"I have brought gifts for you, my lord king of Cortova, and for your family. Will you receive them?"

"With great pleasure. You do us honor."

At Alaric's signal, two knights stepped forward. One held the leather case while the other loosened the drawstring and drew back the velvet covering. Then together they tilted it toward the king so he could admire the glittering bowl.

"This handbasin has been in my family since the reign of King Mortimer. I offer it to you now as a gesture of my esteem."

Gonzalo leaned forward and studied it for a moment, then sat back and smiled at Alaric. "Very handsome," he said, quite rosy with pleasure. "Most generous indeed. I thank you, my lord King Alaric."

The knights now stepped back, still holding the presentation case open and tilted, while the next gift was presented.

"For your son and heir, Prince Castor of Cortova, I wish to present this fine young falcon, trained in our royal mews."

The prince, who had heretofore looked bored, was suddenly wild with interest. "Take off the hood! Take off the hood!" he cried, jumping up from his seat. "I want to see him."

Gonzalo reached out, as cool as a winter breeze, grabbed Castor by the arm, and pulled him back into his chair. He did this without the slightest change of expression, as if his hand wasn't actually a part of him but some servant who did his bidding.

"I thank you on behalf of my son, Prince Castor," he said. "I will see that he is properly trained in the sport of hawking. But for now I believe we had best keep the hood on so as not to startle —"

"But, *Father*!" the prince interrupted, straining against the king's grip, which only grew tighter. "Ow! Stop it! Ow!"

The knight holding the falcon went to stand beside the ones holding the bowl, and the last of the gifts was brought forward.

"And for your daughter, Princess Anna Maria Elizabetta of Cortova, I would like to present this small token of my great admiration."

The princess, who seemed to have an infinite number of faces (all of them beautiful), had worn her regal face today. She sat very still, her back straight, her hands folded in her lap, and her eyes fixed squarely on the king of Westria—as they had been since the moment he'd entered the room. Now as Alaric took the ebony case from his gentleman knight and offered it to her himself—removing the lid, tilting the box so she could see the cup—she let a smile creep onto her lips.

"I thank you most sincerely," Gonzalo said, "on behalf of my daughter, for this exceptional gift. You are too generous."

"Not at all, my lord King Gonzalo. It is my great pleasure. But I wonder if you might grant me one very small favor."

"A favor?" He squinted, suspicious now.

"Yes, my lord king—a very small one, I promise. As I have come to Cortova to ask for the lady's hand in marriage, I would be most honored if she would consent to drink a toast with this cup—a toast to friendship, nothing more. I perfectly understand that no promises are being made. But it would please me enormously if she would."

Gonzalo hesitated for just the briefest moment, still wondering if there was a catch somewhere, a trap, a trick. But apparently he couldn't find one.

"Why not?" he said at last. "A toast to friendship. Where's the harm?"

"Thank you, my lord king, for indulging my little whim."

A bottle of Westria's finest vintage was brought out and opened by one of the knights, who handed it to the king, who poured a little into the beautiful cup and offered it to the princess with a courtly bow.

"My lord King Alaric," she said, "I also wish to thank you for this beautiful cup." Her eyes sparkled as she held the cup aloft. "To everlasting friendship between our two kingdoms," she said. "And between ourselves."

Then she drank from the cup.

And it was done.

Day Five

❦ 19 ❧

On the Ragged Edge

REYNARD WAS NEAR THE breaking point. If he grew any angrier, he feared he might burst into flames. *Blast and double blast! May the king of Cortova die a long and hideous death! May he rot from within and be forced to watch as his bowels were eaten by worms!*

Reynard stopped raging and took a deep breath. This was not constructive.

But by everything that was sacred, it was an outrage: demanding that Reynard sign a paper agreeing to terms that were only half considered and still under discussion, while Gonzalo had to promise nothing—*nothing*—and still might form an alliance with Alaric in the end. Yes, yes, he'd put in a clause about that. But really, what was the point? First you discuss, then you agree—then and *only then* do you put it in writing. That's how things were done.

Had he gotten Alaric to sign a contract, too? Probably. Gonzalo was locking in each and every gain, so there'd be no going back later. And as the talks progressed, with yet more desperate concessions, there'd be *another* temporary contract, and another one after that.

God's blood, but the man was a monster! Really, there was no good outcome whether Reynard won or lost. There had to be a better way.

He now thought for the thousandth time about what his son had seen. Granted, Rupert wasn't famous for his brilliance, but he wasn't a complete loss, either; and the scene he'd described did seem to lead to the conclusions he had drawn. Of course there might be some other explanation, but Reynard couldn't think what it might be. So just for the sake of argument, what if the boy was right for the first time in his life, and Gonzalo wasn't as rich as he appeared?

It was worth exploring.

First, as Gonzalo himself had pointed out, he'd never wanted an alliance before because it would be bad for business. So why did he want one now? Point one for Rupert.

Second, Gonzalo had made a conspicuous display of his great wealth: Midas of the Peninsula, Colossus of the Southern Sea! Yet he hadn't paid the bloody entertainers.

Once again, Rupert had hit the mark by noting that Gonzalo already *had* the silver plates, the antique cups, the candlesticks, and all the rest. They'd been hanging around the palace for generations. That didn't mean he was rich now.

And yet another astute question his son had raised: Why hadn't he given a second banquet in Alaric's honor? Was it possible that he'd planned his spectacle for both of them; but the party from Westria had come a day late, and he *couldn't afford to repeat it*?

If so then he'd lured both kings into signing documents agreeing to hand over great piles of gold in exchange for—nothing! Yet he couldn't walk away because, if he was wrong, Alaric would get everything and Austlind would be lost.

A devil of a situation! *Blast and double blast!*

At least one thing was certain: he'd have to stop discounting that boy of his. With a little more attention and a firmer hand, young Rupert might grow up to be a half-intelligent human being. Certainly he'd put his finger on the problem and come up with the only real solution.

Except that Reynard didn't think he could bring himself to kill his cousin, however much was at stake. He was a king, not a murderer.

Now, if it came to war between Austlind and Westria and he and Alaric should meet on the battlefield, that would be an entirely different matter. Reynard wouldn't hesitate to cut down the boy—even knowing in his heart that it wasn't a fair fight, that Alaric was young and untested and hadn't even finished his training. Reynard would do it because they were at war, and he was fighting for the life's blood of Austlind.

Was it really so different now?

No. It was exactly the same.

But then—by the saints, was there no end to the complications?—there was that bloody silver bowl. Was it really cursed? Those wolves at the banquet had been pretty damned convincing. Yet no harm had come to Alaric since, so maybe . . .

Oh, blast it all, his brain was tired. How was he supposed to make a decision when he didn't have all the facts? Well, he'd just have to make his best judgment and hope that it was right.

That was, after all, what being a king was all about.

Part Four

Attack—an aggressive move or series of moves.

Check—the act of attacking the opponent's king.

Illegal move—a move made contrary to the rules of the game.

Day Six and Beyond

❦ 20 ❧

Poison

THAT EVENING, AS ALARIC was dressing for dinner, he'd begun to feel unwell. He had taken a bite from the slice of berry cake that was on the tray beside his jug of wine. Minutes later, he became nauseous. His physician, Polonius, had begged him not to go to that night's dinner.

But Alaric had refused. He could not afford to offend Gonzalo, especially since "not feeling well" was the most time-worn excuse in the world. Also, it would give Reynard an advantage. So, true to his nature, he had soldiered on. He'd gone to the dinner and had even tried to swallow a few bites.

Then suddenly it had hit him hard: a sharp pain in the gut combined with nausea, dizziness, and shortness of breath. Molly, who was beside him on the dining couch, had seen him flinch and heard him gasp. Without being too obvious, she'd touched his arm and asked in a whisper if he was all right.

"No," he'd said.

"Shall we leave?"

"Yes."

Molly had turned to Tobias then, and things were said, and after that people were getting up and doing something; but to Alaric it had all been a blur. He was pretty sure he'd walked out on his own two feet—well, Tobias had helped considerably—but he knew he'd been carried the rest of the way. Beyond that he remembered nothing.

When he came to himself again he was in bed in his own chamber, and the lamp-lit face of Polonius was gazing down at him out of the darkness. The physician seemed to be examining his eyes. He nodded, grunted, and sat back.

"Your Highness," he said in greeting, as in, "Welcome back to the land of the living."

Molly was there, along with Heptor Brochton and

several other knights and also a couple of pages. Far too many bodies in one small chamber. It was stuffy, he noticed, and it stank of vomit.

"I'm hot," he said, but it came out more like "Immaa." He tried again and did somewhat better this time.

"Pull back the coverlet," the physician told one of the pages. "Your Majesty, can you tell me how you feel?" He laid a firm hand on the king's belly. "Any pain here?"

Alaric had to think about it. How, actually, would one define *pain*? He certainly felt like a corpse that had been hauled up out of its grave and miraculously brought back to life. But the sensation of being stabbed in the gut . . . no, he wasn't feeling that anymore. Just kind of a dull ache, along with a sort of burning and a throbbing in the head . . .

"My lord?"

"Unh. Unh. I don't . . . um . . . I'm a little better."

The physician had his wrist now and was feeling his pulse.

"What happened?"

"You are ill, Your Majesty."

Well, he knew *that*, for heaven's sake! He closed his eyes and had a private little conversation with his body. There were a lot of complaints.

"Would you like to tell me a bit more?" Alaric said, rather reassured by the tone of his voice now. It had the ring of authority, though it was certainly weak.

"Are you sure you wouldn't rather wait till tomorrow to discuss it? You've had quite a time of it, you know."

"Yes, I do know. And yes, I want to discuss it."

"Well then, if you insist, it appears that you have been poisoned."

Alaric's drooping eyes flew open. "Poisoned? Are you sure?"

"Quite. The signs were clear."

"What signs?"

"Well, all of them: nausea and vomiting, accelerated heart rate, rapid breathing, red splotches on your skin, sharp pain in the belly, unconsciousness. And then, of course, there was the greenish cast of the vomitus."

"*My* vomitus?"

"Yes, Your Majesty."

"You studied my vomit?"

"Yes, Your Majesty. One always does in such cases."

This was far too much for the king to absorb. He closed his eyes again.

"You will continue to take my powders throughout the night. They're very bland, and we mix them with honey, so they won't be hard to get down. I also want you to drink plenty of fluids. I'm afraid we'll have to wake you now and again, but it's imperative that you stay on an exact regimen."

"Who?" the king asked.

"Who? *I* shall wake you, Your Highness. I shall be right here and will not leave your—"

"No—who *poisoned* me?"

"Oh. Excuse me. I misunderstood. Well, Your Majesty, we only have theories, and it's always best not to jump to—"

"Reynard," said Heptor Brochton.

Alaric looked up at Heptor. "Why? How?"

"As to the *why*, he probably got tired of King Gonzalo's nonsense and decided to solve his problem the easy way."

"Sounds logical."

"Yes, it does, Your Majesty. As to the *how*, I would guess he bribed a slave to put something in your food."

"The cake."

"What cake?" Polonius asked.

"Berry cake; it came with the wine. I didn't eat much. It was bloody awful."

"Well, there's no sign of it now," Heptor said. "The slaves must have taken it away."

"That explains the red flecks in the vomitus," Polonius added thoughtfully.

Alaric ardently wished they would all stop talking and go away, but there seemed little hope of that. So he let his gaze drift over to Molly, who stood quietly in the back of the room.

"I don't want her to leave," he said. The physician leaned in to hear him. Alaric's words had gone all mumbly again.

"Excuse me, Your Grace?"

"Molly."

"The lady?"

"Tell her to stay."

"Ah. Well, perhaps she can come again tomorrow, Your Majesty—how would that be? After she's had a bit of sleep, in her own guesthouse, with the other women as is fitting. It is late, Your Highness. I'm sure she's very tired."

"Of course," he murmured. "Tomorrow."

He shut his eyes and felt himself drifting off again.

His breathing was deep and steady now: in, out; in, out; in, out.

"That's it, my lord. A nice long rest is exactly what you need. You'll feel better in the morning."

❦ 21 ❦

More Green Than Rosy

ALARIC RECOVERED MORE QUICKLY than expected.
But he was still weak, and his mind wasn't nearly sharp
enough to tangle with Gonzalo again. So he kept to his
rooms for a few more days.

There had been a steady stream of inquiries from
the palace, which Heptor answered according to Alaric's directions. The princess sent several very short,
very beautifully written notes of condolence, along
with a large bowl of flowers from her garden. King
Gonzalo had begged to know the gravity of Alaric's
condition and offered the services of his own physician, who was world renowned and had formerly

served the sultan of Kaldar.

Heptor had thanked them both for their kind concern. The king of Westria had been struck by a sudden attack of the flux, but he was already feeling better. And while he appreciated King Gonzalo's offer, Alaric always traveled with his own physician and was being well taken care of. The king of Westria did apologize, however, for the delay in the negotiations. He hoped it wouldn't be too much of an inconvenience.

The king of Cortova had replied that Alaric was not to worry; it wasn't inconvenient at all. The king of Westria must take all the time he needed to recover from his regrettable illness. Then, as soon as he was quite himself again, they would all celebrate his return to health with a jolly little hunting party, as previously planned. A day outdoors with lots of fresh air and sunshine was just what was needed to put the roses back in the king of Westria's cheeks.

"The man is mad," Alaric had said upon hearing this. "He wants me to go *hunting*—to put the *roses back in my cheeks*? Please, someone, poison me again!"

"Why do you suppose?" Heptor had asked. "It *is* peculiar."

"I can't imagine, except that it must be part of his grand design. Perhaps he's had a stag dipped in gold and put fairies up in the trees with lutes, and he just can't bear to waste all that effort."

"Sounds about right."

"Any hope of getting out of the hunt altogether? We could say I can't ride because I've lost the use of my legs."

"Are you serious?"

"*No*, Heptor, I'm not serious! Have you no sense of humor at all?"

"No, my lord. Never did. But I'm glad you have and that you've found it again. I take that as a very good sign."

⚮

Molly had returned, as promised, the morning after Alaric's collapse and had since spent her days in the king's villa. But she was usually to be found in some odd corner of the room, standing quietly while the others bustled about, fussing and fretting and telling the king what to do: "Take another spoonful of this pasty, insipid gruel, Your Highness." "Have another dose of powdered chalk, glopped up with honey, my lord." "Please take a sip of watered wine with strange, unpleasant additives, Your Majesty." Or when they were offering him none of these things, "Have a nice little rest, Your Majesty." It had been impossible for him to speak with her in private.

Then one day he reminded himself that *he* was the king and sent the whole lot of them out of the room; he wanted a moment alone with his friend, the lady Marguerite. Subtle looks of disapproval were exchanged by one and all, but there was no denying his request (though the physician privately urged her not to stay too long).

"Well, Molly," he said as she pulled a chair up to the bedside and sat down, "I must say you're looking very grim. An outside observer would be hard pressed to tell which of us was the suffering patient and which the visiting friend, except that I'm in bed and you are not."

She didn't laugh.

"Oh, for heaven's sake," he complained. "I'm surrounded by morose people. Can't you manage a smile? Look at me: the very picture of rosy health!"

"On the contrary, Alaric. You're as bony as a peasant's hen, there are dark circles under your eyes, and your complexion is more green than rosy."

"Thank you. I feel much better now."

"This is serious, Alaric. You might have died!"

"And that's supposed to be my fault?"

"No. Apparently Reynard's."

"So everyone seems to agree."

"You don't believe it?"

"Almost," he said. "Not quite."

"Then tell me why."

"I *almost* believe it because he's the obvious person, the only one who stands to gain. He's trapped in an impossible situation—we both are—and my death would bring him release. He'd inherit my throne, grow twice as strong, and have no further need of an alliance with Cortova."

"And?"

"I *don't quite* believe it for the same reason: because he's the obvious person. He has to know that he'd be suspected of having me poisoned. His reputation would be destroyed, and that would trouble him greatly, as he is a proud man. Moreover, if he was publicly suspected of poisoning me, Westria would never accept him as king. Lord Mayhew would rise against him with the full force of the army. Reynard is smarter than that."

"Maybe he was just desperate enough to do it anyway."

"There's another thing, Molly. My cousin is a hard and a ruthless man, but he's not without principles. Where exactly he draws his lines has long been a mystery to me, but I can't see him stooping to bribing a slave to poison my food. He would consider it low, demeaning."

"Well, someone did it."

"Yes. And no one else has a motive. It's a puzzle."

"Are you really going to join Gonzalo's hunting party?"

"It's right up there with inspecting vomitus on my list of amusing things to do."

"Then don't go. It isn't wise. Whoever tried to kill you before will most likely try again. It's someone here in Cortova, at least we know that much; and that someone will almost surely go on the hunt."

"Or he'll stay behind if I do and kill me while everyone's away."

"Oh, Alaric. Won't you please listen to reason?"

"I never do, Molly. Haven't you noticed?"

Day Twelve

❦ 22 ❦

The Hunt

THEY SET OUT EARLY, in the full dark of early morning. Gonzalo and his courtiers had laid their togas aside for the occasion and wore doublets and hose like everybody else. All were equipped as if for battle: mounted on coursers, armed with bows and arrows, the gentlemen carrying swords, and everyone wearing hunting horns that hung low from baldrics strapped across their chests.

A little before sunrise, they arrived at the king's hunting park. Huntsmen and dogs were already milling about, and liveried grooms stood ready to take their horses. A trestle table, draped in forest-green linen and covered with a lavish spread of dishes, had been set up in a clearing so the guests could break their fasts. And carpets had been laid out on the ground, on which were many little stools for the hunters and their ladies to sit upon. In keeping with the rustic setting, they were to serve themselves and would eat their meal off wooden trenchers.

Tobias had been looking forward to this hunt, mostly because it would give him a chance to be with Molly. He hadn't seen her since the night the king had collapsed, and he'd stored up a vast quantity of things he wanted to discuss with her. But in this she had disappointed him. Though they'd ridden side by side for nigh on two hours, Molly had said hardly a word. And now as they sat side by side in the clearing, trenchers of food on their laps, she was just as quiet and withdrawn.

Molly was troubled, that was clear enough. But in the past she'd shared her worries with him. Over the years, in one dangerous situation after another, they'd worked out a plan together: each spotting problems the other had missed till they arrived at a good conclusion. So whatever burden she carried now—and Tobias was pretty sure he knew—there seemed no point in her carrying it alone.

He turned to catch her eye, but she was looking

elsewhere. So Tobias followed her gaze and saw—no surprise—that she was watching Alaric.

The king stood some distance away, leaning against the trunk of a tree, talking with the princess. He'd always been slight; but now he was gaunt, almost frail, and it passed through Tobias's mind that he might not be recovered at all. Perhaps the physician had been mistaken in his diagnosis or his treatment.

The princess now leaned closer to Alaric—smiling and looking down and to the side, as one does when saying something wicked or when making a clever remark that has a private quality to it—and Alaric's face lit up with amusement. Then she raised her eyes and met his directly, apparently proud of her own wit and eager to have his response. He gave it to her in the form of a warm smile. Then she said something else, and he just listened, gazing at her so fixedly that you'd think she was in danger of disappearing should he forget himself and look away.

Tobias found this fascinating to watch. It was as if the two were entirely alone, not surrounded by near a hundred people. And then he remembered: of course! Alaric had given her the cup.

What a terrible decision that must have been for the king to make: binding himself to someone with a love that would never end when he had no assurance they could actually be together. Gonzalo didn't care about his daughter's feelings, however ardent they might be. The lady and the treaty would go to the highest bidder. And if that turned out to be Reynard, then Alaric would have to watch as his beloved was carted off to Austlind to marry that lack-wit, Prince Rupert. Horrible for him and horrible for her—on top of losing the alliance.

Now Tobias looked at the couple again with all of this in mind, curious to see what undying love was like and whether affection wrought by magic was different from the ordinary kind. But he saw nothing dramatic—just two people happy to be together, interested in what the other had to say and eager to be amused.

And judging from Tobias's own experience, that's what love was all about: comfort and friendship, trust and ease, little jokes, loyalty, devotion, and understanding. The only difference was that in the real world, you really had to know a person before you could love her. And that took time—months, even years of being together in all sorts of different situations. Gradually it crept up on you, the sense that somehow this person had become essential to your happiness and that you would do anything to protect her, no matter what the cost. Did Alaric and Elizabetta have all that too, he wondered—instantly and unearned?

He turned back to Molly. This time she noticed.

"Will you ride?" he asked. "Or stay here with Lady Eleanor and Lady Claire?"

"I'll ride."

He nodded. He'd expected she would, not out of any interest in the hunt but because she sensed the king might be in danger and hoped that somehow, if she was there, she might be able to protect him. Tobias agreed with this decision. She needed to go. All the same, he was as worried about her safety as he was about Alaric's.

Molly was not a skilled rider. Long trudges through the countryside were one thing, but she didn't feel comfortable at a gallop. And this hunt would be unlike anything in her experience. It would be a crush of horses and men, with caution thrown to the winds in the excitement of the chase. Unless Alaric hung back to an extraordinary degree, there was no way she could keep up with him. And if she tried to do so, she would put her life at risk.

"Molly," he said, "we need a plan."

"Such as?"

"Something that doesn't involve your being trampled by horses."

"Ah."

"Go at your own pace and stay away from the racers. You'll know right away who they are. They'll have this wild look about them, as if the world's going to end if they don't get to the stag first. I swear it's a form of madness. They'll ram you and knock you out of your saddle without even noticing they've done it."

"But there's no point in riding at all if I'm too far behind to warn Alaric if something's going to happen. The whole reason—"

"No, Molly, listen. We can do it together. I can easily stay at his side. If you sense so much as a whiff of danger, blow your horn. I'll do the rest. And you can concentrate better on listening for a warning if you're not terrified of being thrown off your mount."

She took up her horn with a hint of amusement and pretended to blow it. "Like this?"

"Exactly so, only louder. That is to say, making an actual sound."

"Thank you, Tobias. I'll keep that in mind."

She was grinning now, almost playful, and Tobias felt relief wash over him. These last few weeks Molly had become overwhelmed by fear and dread. And this was a problem, not just because it made her unhappy, but because it made her weak. She'd lost that remarkable combination of fierce toughness and reckless self-assurance that had carried her victorious through every kind of danger. And if there was ever a time when she was going to need it, that time was now. How wonderful, then, to see the light return to her eyes and to recognize the old, familiar Molly.

"Just blow the horn," he said again, "and I'll protect him with my life."

"I know you will." She took his hand and squeezed it. "We always were a good team," she said.

⚓

In the time since Tobias had been made a lord, he'd done a bit of hunting, so he thought he knew what to expect. You found a stag, you flushed him out of his hiding place, then you thundered after him, your hounds at his heels, until someone managed to take him. Or, alternatively, you ran him to the point of exhaustion, making it an easy shot, generally reserved for the host or an honored guest.

But a royal hunt, he now realized, was something altogether different. It was a spectacle, as complicated and carefully planned as the assembling of an army for battle. In addition to the usual men and horses, you needed a small battalion of dogs of varying breeds, each highly trained in a particular skill: gaze hounds, scent hounds, and running hounds. All were accompanied by expert handlers, one for every two dogs, who placed them exactly where they needed to be to do what they needed to do and let them loose at just the right moment.

In addition to the dog handlers, the king's hunting staff included horn blowers, archers, a chief huntsman and his many subordinates, twenty sergeants of the hunt, and a host of pages and grooms. All were identically dressed in caped hoods of forest green— presumably so they would blend in with the trees.

And as with any army, there must first be reconnaissance: advance men who gathered information. In this case, it was the king's gamekeeper, who'd gone out into the forest days before to track down a stag he deemed worthy of a royal hunt, after which he'd kept a close watch so as not to lose him before the king and his guests arrived.

As everyone in Cortova must know by now (for Gonzalo had not stopped talking about it since the moment they arrived), the gamekeeper's quest had led him to an enormous hart, or male red deer, with a rack of fourteen tines.

The stag was now harbored in a fern thicket. And as soon as everything and everyone was in place, he'd be driven out by the first relay of hounds, sent along a path of the huntsmen's devising. Sergeants would be stationed along the way to keep him on course as he fled from the baying hounds and the host of hunters who pursued him through the forest.

King Gonzalo, together with his knights, Prince Castor, and the princess Elizabetta, would be positioned at the end of the run, the choice spot for making the kill. Alaric had volunteered to wait farther up the line—a less desirable place, as it meant almost no chance of taking the hart (and a lot more running for the horses). This had been a gesture of courtesy, and Gonzalo had taken it as such. But in truth, Alaric didn't care whether he killed the stag or not. He just wanted to stay alive, get this day over with, go back to the summer palace and finish the blasted negotiations, then return to Westria, where he could hunt in peace in his own forest any old time he liked.

They were assembled now, waiting for the hunt to begin. From somewhere in the distance a horn gave the signal that the handlers had let slip the dogs. Now a raucous baying of hounds rose up as the stag was driven out of cover, followed by the rumble of hooves as the first relay of hunters began the chase. Alaric's party waited their turn, keeping a tight rein on their restless mounts and fixedly watching the path where—soon, very soon—the hart would come dashing by.

But Tobias was turned in the opposite direction, scanning the trees, alert to any movement, any patch of color that didn't belong in a forest. He knew how easy it would be for an assassin to slip up behind them while everyone was looking for the stag. But he saw nothing—or nothing yet.

Tobias turned to Molly, and she nodded in understanding, a deep furrow between her brows. She'd sensed it at the exact same moment he had: The knights had been seduced by the thrill of the chase. They'd forgotten they were there to protect the king.

The tension was rising now. The knights, and even Alaric, were almost breathless with anticipation: muscles taut, senses tuned, ready to spring into action the moment the hart came into view. Their coursers danced in place, eager and impatient, as the sounds of the approaching pack grew louder and louder. And then, with astonishing suddenness, the noble hart—with his beautiful russet coat and great rack of antlers—passed them in a blur of motion, leaping with incredible grace, his hooves striking the hard-packed earth like the beat of a drum. And not far behind him came the dogs and the first relay of mounted hunters.

In an instant the king and his men were off, joining the melee, and Tobias was close behind. Now he urged his mount forward through that crush of men and horses and made slow but steady headway till he reached Alaric's side. There he stayed, alert for any sign of danger.

But that didn't keep him from worrying about Molly. For a royal hunt was not just grander than the ones on his neighbors' estates; it was also a lot more dangerous. There were many more riders, for one thing. And they weren't just a bunch of country gentlemen out for a day of sport; most of them were knights, trained to ride into battle. They were aggressive, fearless, and wild with excitement. You didn't want to get in their way.

The terrain was trickier, too. The path was uneven, and while it was broad in places, it would occasionally grow narrower. So the pack would spread out, then come together again. And in the midst of all that, even if Molly kept clear of the wildest racers, she could still be thrown off balance. Or another rider, pressing too close as he passed, might pull her boot out of the stirrup. However it happened, if she were to fall, she'd be trampled by the horde that followed.

More than anything, Tobias wanted to turn back and make sure that she was all right. But he'd promised to stay by Alaric and keep him safe, so that's what he did. And he was just noting, with some concern, how exhausted the king looked when he heard the sharp blast of a horn.

Neither Molly nor Tobias had realized when they'd made their plan that there'd be so many horns being blown in the chase. There was apparently a whole language of signals, familiar to everyone but them. There might be one blast, or two, or three. They might be quick, or long and sustained. One might mean "all assemble," while another sent the dogs on the chase, and a third encouraged them to run faster. No doubt there was also a call of distress and a different one to say that the stag had left the path and was taking an unexpected route.

But this particular blast was like none of the others. It sounded like a girl who'd never blown a hunting horn before but was desperate to get someone's attention.

"Alaric!" Tobias screamed. "Watch out!"

Even as he cried the warning, an arrow came singing out of the underbrush. Tobias reached out instinctively to pull the king down, but it was already too late. The arrow, perfectly aimed, was coming too fast.

Then, in the fraction of a second that remained before that deadly missile hit its mark, its shaft began to bend, curving upward, tracing an arc that sent it flying over Alaric's head, higher and higher, until it bit with tremendous force into the trunk of an ancient pine.

Lord Brochton and a few other knights dashed headlong into the trees, determined to flush out the assassin. The rest reined in their horses, causing a crush as more came thundering in from behind. The air filled with shouts and curses.

"What the devil?" someone cried. "What's going on?"

"The king! The king! Is he wounded?"

"Look! That's the arrow, right there! Did you ever see the like? Bent like a bloody sickle!"

Alaric and his party quickly turned off the path and made their way warily through the forest until they'd reached the clearing. There, the knights formed a human shield around him, all of them facing out, their weapons drawn, and waited for Lord Brochton and his men to return.

They came back half an hour later, scowling. The archer had escaped. But they'd found King Gonzalo farther down the line, and he'd immediately sent out a score of men with scent hounds to scour the forest. The greater numbers, plus the addition of dogs, would certainly make the task easier. Perhaps they would find the man.

Meanwhile, Lord Brochton didn't think it wise to stay in the park any longer. He suggested they leave immediately for the safer and more controlled environment of the palace. Alaric wholeheartedly agreed.

So they mounted their coursers and headed south, the king once again surrounded by a tight formation of knights. This made them all feel better, though they knew they couldn't protect him like that every minute of every day. Alaric had business to do; he had to meet with King Gonzalo and attend royal dinners. And every time he left his villa he put himself at risk.

Whoever it was that wanted him dead would likely try again. The next time he might succeed.

Day Thirteen

❦ 23 ❦

Illegal Move

MOLLY HAD MADE PLANS for this morning, the first real time she'd had to herself since Alaric had fallen ill.

For better or worse, he had gone off to the palace to resume the negotiations. Molly (and pretty much everyone else) had argued strongly against this. The king had been poisoned, then nearly skewered by an arrow, and all in the course of a week. He needed to rest and gather his wits before facing Gonzalo again. But Alaric had waved away their caution. He had to get the business over with as soon as he possibly could. He was afraid that if he dragged it out a single day longer, he might go completely mad, and that wouldn't help with the negotiations either.

Molly had to agree; this was a very good point. And anyway, there was nothing she could do to change his mind. So she took her free morning as a gift and planned to use it well. Alaric might not need time to pull his wits together, but she certainly did.

The cat had returned the night before.

⚜

"The game of chess is governed by a set of laws," he'd said.

He was on the marble railing again, pacing back and forth with some agitation; she'd been amazed by how delicately he'd made the turns, considering his immense size.

"I know," she'd replied.

"If a player moves a piece in a way that is contrary to those laws, it's called an illegal move."

"Are we talking about moves that have already been made or moves that are yet to come?"

"The game isn't over. It grows more difficult now."

"Oh, please, Leondas—tell me something useful!"

"Remember what Sigrid said: your spirit will tell you what you need to know when you need to know it."

"Is that it, then?"

"You have defeated a powerful opponent before," he said. "Now you must do it again."

⁂

None of this had really come as a surprise to Molly. It just affirmed what she was already feeling—that the forces that had been gathering, like clouds before a storm, were poised and ready to strike. It wouldn't be long now; and when it came, much would be demanded of her. What exactly she'd be called upon to do she had no earthly idea; her spirit didn't think she needed to know. But at least she had this moment of calm to prepare. She'd take a walk in the garden, find herself a quiet place to sit, and try to get herself under control.

And then, just as she was imagining it, her little gift was snatched away. A note arrived from the princess, inviting her to come and play chess. It was graciously written, but it was a summons all the same. Molly had no choice but to go.

And who could tell—perhaps the summons had come not just from the princess of Cortova, but from Molly's own spirit as well.

⁂

They took their usual places across from each other—Molly playing white, Betta playing black. And according to the rules of chess, white must begin.

Molly brought out one of her middle pawns—two squares, as was allowed on the first move. Now she waited for the princess to take her turn.

The door to the royal bedchamber had been left open, and for some reason Molly felt drawn to look inside. There was a gilt table against the far wall with a bowl of flowers on it. And beside the flowers she saw the Loving Cup.

Molly's heart did something strange in her chest: a leap followed by a twitch.

The princess was waiting. She'd also moved a middle pawn two squares. Now the two pieces stood face-to-face.

"Remember that pawns can only capture diagonally," Betta said, "and can only move straight ahead."

"So we're stuck."

"These two are, for the moment."

Molly stared at the board for a while, but she wasn't thinking about chess.

"Were you pleased with King Alaric's gift?" she asked, still looking down fixedly. When her question was greeted with silence, and that silence went on for an uncomfortably long time, Molly raised her eyes. Betta's expression—probing, curious, slightly amused—made her squirm.

"Alaric . . . the king showed it to me," Molly stammered. "Before, you know . . . Well, I mean, I thought the cup was so very handsome. And I just wondered . . ."

"Yes," the princess said. "I liked his gift very much."

Molly let out the breath she'd been holding, then sucked in more air. "He was hoping you'd drink a toast—"

"To friendship, yes. That was very *elegant* of him."

"And did you? Drink a toast?"

The princess was grinning now. "Why, of course," she said. "Did he not tell you?"

"He was preoccupied; we had no occasion to discuss it. But I'm glad you did. I'm sure it pleased him. And he's a good man, deserving of your kindness."

"I know that."

Molly felt her face flash hot with embarrassment and shame. Could she possibly have been more clumsy and transparent?

She looked down at the two pawns standing face-to-face and took a deep breath.

"What should I do now?" she asked. "I mean, what should my next move be?"

Oh for heaven's sake, she thought, blushing again. Everything that came out of her mouth seemed to carry some embarrassing double meaning. And the truth was, she really didn't know what her next move should be—with the princess *or* in the game.

"How about your knight?" Betta said, kindly ignoring Molly's discomfiture. "Take a look. Can he help you?"

Molly stared, mentally projecting the knight's odd L-shaped pattern of movement onto the board. "Oh," she said. "If I move this one out, he'll be in place to capture your pawn."

"Good. Go ahead."

Molly did, feeling a brief moment of triumph—until Betta brought out her own knight, mirroring Molly's move. So if Molly captured Betta's pawn, Betta would take her knight.

"We're stuck again," she said.

"Yes, but the board has changed. Your move."

Molly focused hard. Then she saw her chance and moved her bishop—one square, two squares, three squares. As matters stood now, unless the princess sacrificed her knight by moving him into the bishop's path, Molly could take one of her pawns and would be in position to threaten her king.

"Well played! Isn't this fun?"

Molly rubbed her chin, thinking how to answer.

"I like stretching my brain," she said. "And it's fun

when I come up with something clever, as I did just now. But it's also bloody hard. I know you'll just counter my wonderful move with a better one of your own so that I'll be in danger again. And it'll go on like that, getting harder and more complicated with every move, until—"

"Until the game is over," Betta said. "So very like what's going on around us now."

Molly stopped breathing.

"Don't look so amazed. We can be plain with each other."

"Can we?"

"Of course."

"And you never say anything you don't really mean."

Betta smiled and gave the faintest nod.

Molly sat up straighter now and looked squarely at the princess. "Then tell me honestly—how will it end? And I'm not referring to chess."

"I don't know. I rather thought *you* might."

"Me? Why ever would you think such a thing?"

For once the princess seemed at a loss for words. "It's just something I've heard," she tried, clearly not pleased with her effort. "Forgive me, Molly, but people say you have a gift for seeing the future."

"What people? We're being plain, remember?"

"My father's spies, who heard the stories in Westria."

"Well, thank you for your honesty."

"And yesterday, when that attempt was made on Alaric's life, there were some around you who said you behaved strangely. They swear you saw that arrow in your mind before it even flew and that it was you who changed its course and saved your king from certain death."

"People say all sorts of ridiculous things."

"So they do. Just a fairy tale, then? No truth to it at all?"

"Betta, did you invite me here today so you could ask that question?"

Once again the princess struggled to find an answer. "Not entirely," she finally said, "and not so blatantly as you make it sound. I genuinely wanted your company; I've missed seeing you this past week. But I also hoped the stories were true and that as my friend, you would tell me what the future holds. My life hangs in the balance, you see."

"Wouldn't you do better to ask your father?"

She dismissed this with a bitter laugh.

"Well, I'm afraid I can't tell you, either, because I

don't know what's going to happen. And that's God's honest truth."

"Oh, well," she said, cocking her head to one side and gazing up at the sky.

"If *you* knew the answer," Molly went on, still working on the thought as a dog worries a bone, "if you were privy to your father's intentions or had found it out by using your magical powers—would you tell *me*? My life hangs in the balance too."

The princess turned back to Molly, an odd expression on her face.

"Let me ask it another way. Are we friends or opponents?"

"We are both."

"I see."

"All I do, I do for the good of Cortova. You do the same for Westria. So our goals are not exactly the same."

"Fair enough."

"But I am also your friend. And if I knew how this game was going to end—and I could tell you without betraying my country—then whatever else it might cost me, I would tell you."

On impulse, Molly reached across the board and took the princess's hand. "I believe you," she said.

The cat was waiting in the garden as she passed through on her way out. She almost laughed when she saw him, for *of course* he would be there. Everything around her was alive with portent. She could almost *hear* the wheels of fate grinding away, every small moment of every passing day bringing her closer and closer to that secret future in which there would be things that she could change and others she could not because they were written in the stars. And she was right on the cusp of it now; she could feel it in her bones.

As in her vision, the cat seemed distressed. He danced around her as she walked, nosing at her ankles and getting in her way. It was as if he wanted her to stop, as if he wanted to tell her something. So Molly squatted down and scratched him behind the ears. "What is it, Leondas?" she crooned.

But he couldn't answer, of course, and he didn't want to be petted. He pulled away and began to circle her, rubbing up against her and stroking her with his tail. Curious and uneasy, Molly remained as she was, squatting on the walk and watching the cat. And in the silence that followed she heard something: a rustle in the bushes, then the slap of sandals on stone. Someone besides the cat had been hiding in the garden;

now that person was running away.

Molly rose and followed the sound. She wasn't sure why, except that her senses thrummed with danger and her instincts pressed her forward. Down the covered walkway she went, thinking strategically. She was nearing the point where the colonnade took a turn to the right, beyond which, of course, she couldn't see. So she slowed her pace, kept hard to the left so she'd have a better angle of observation, and prepared herself to fight.

When she reached the corner, Molly paused, scanning frantically with her eyes. Then she saw him and melted with relief. For there in the shadows, leaning against a wall, looking very small and not the least bit threatening, was young Prince Castor.

He had a furtive look about him and seemed to be holding something behind his back. Molly guessed that he'd been spying on his sister and had probably stolen from her as well. Neither would surprise her. Castor was an odd little boy. Unnatural, possibly even disturbed. Spying and stealing were just the sort of things he would do.

Still, it was awkward. He was the crown prince of Cortova, and Molly was just a guest—a guest who didn't wish to offend the royal family and make trouble for her own king. So she dropped a nice curtsy, said, "Good morning, Prince Castor," and continued on her way. But before she'd taken two steps, the boy had moved away from the wall and now stood directly in her path. Instantly, Molly's defenses went up again.

"Excuse me," she said, trying to step around him; but he moved again to block her. Angry now, she made a scolding face, as nursemaids do to naughty children. Castor shot back a look of such unvarnished malice that she had to remind herself that he couldn't really hurt her, that he was just a nasty, spoiled little child who'd been caught doing mischief.

All the same, she needed to get away.

So she made a quick move, darting around him and sprinting down the corridor, half afraid he would come after her and a bit concerned that the thing he'd been hiding might have been a knife. But there were no following footfalls, only silence.

When she reached the safety of the gate, Molly looked back to see if he was still there. And so he was, exactly where she'd left him, except that he'd turned around to watch her run away. And he was grinning now in a demented way that said he knew something, that the joke would be on her, and *wouldn't she be sorry!*

It chilled her to the bone.

She had just arrived at the door to her villa and was about to go inside when something told her to turn around and look at the royal compound. That's when she saw it: a delicate plume of smoke rising in the air.

✤ 24 ✤

Fire

ESTELLA PUT AWAY THE chess set and prepared the
table for the princess's midday meal. As always, there
was a bowl of fruit from the palace orchards. The main
course was squab, poached with figs. And the wine,
brought to the table in an antique ceramic flagon, had
been well watered and chilled, the way her mistress
liked it.

The flagon came with a matching cup, but Estella
had decided to take a chance and put out the fancy
new goblet instead. It was too formal for a simple afternoon meal eaten alone in the garden, and the princess
would probably scold her. But it was such a *very pretty*

thing, and a gift from the lady's suitor (the handsome one, not the pudgy boy with the strange, pale-colored eyes). It seemed positively criminal to have such a treasure and not to use it. If Estella had been given such a beautiful cup (and by such a beautiful man)—why, she'd use it every chance she got. She'd rinse her teeth with it in the mornings!

As it happened, the princess didn't scold her. She just laughed, muttering something about bringing out the gold platters, too, while she was at it, then waved Estella away. The slave smiled with satisfaction, having gotten her way for once. Then she went to stand with Giulia against the far wall, as they always did when the princess dined, or entertained guests, or played chess—always at a discreet distance, where they would be beyond notice yet near enough to be ready at hand should anything be needed.

Estella thought the princess seemed distracted. She got that way sometimes—moodylike—but far more often of late. She was even ignoring Leondas, who was trying very hard to get her attention. Probably thinking about her suitors, Estella decided, that must be it—though what there was to think about, she couldn't imagine. The choice was obvious.

Giulia leaned over and whispered into her ear, "Do you smell something?"

Estella sniffed. "Smoke from the kitchen," she said. "Are you sure?"

Estella shrugged.

They continued to stand as they were, backs to the wall, hands clasped in front. The princess continued to pick at her food and ignore the cat, who now rose up on his hind legs and pawed at his mistress's elbow. How she could fail to notice these attentions was impossible to imagine—and yet she did. She had that look on her face she sometimes got when she was working out a move on the chessboard, as if her mind was completely engaged to the exclusion of everything else.

The garden was uncommonly quiet all of a sudden. Even the birds that nested in the vines had fallen still. In the eerie silence they could hear only the unending, faraway rush of waves on the shore far below—and a strange, crackling sound.

"You're wrong," whispered Giulia. "It's not the kitchen at all. It smells different—sharplike—and it's getting stronger."

Estella sniffed and nodded. "What do you suppose?"

"Don't know. But we ought to mention it, don't you think?"

"Yes. You do it."

So Giulia stepped forward and waited to be acknowledged by her mistress.

"What is it, Giulia?" the princess finally said.

"Please excuse the interruption, my lady, but I'm smelling smoke; and I thought I should call it to your attention."

Elizabetta sniffed the air, then sniffed again.

"Yes, I smell it too," she said, rising quickly from her chair. "Send Estella to see what she can find out and have her report back to me. You go and wake Claudia. I need her right away."

Giulia hurried to the servants' quarters and knocked sharply on Claudia's door. When no answer came, she went in uninvited. Claudia was her superior, a freedwoman, not a slave, so normally she wouldn't have dared to do such a thing. But this was an emergency—and Giulia was secretly glad to have an excuse to wake her up.

"Beg your pardon," she said, "but Mistress wants you. It seems there's a fire somewhere about."

The old woman came to life as Lazarus rose from the dead. Without uttering a single word or even bothering to put on her sandals, she sprinted toward the princess's rooms like a girl of eighteen. Then Giulia hurried off to join the search for the source of the smoke. As she rounded the corner to the hallway that led to the entry gate, she ran headlong into Estella, on her way back. One glance down the hallway was enough to tell Giulia just how bad it was. The palace was old and the beams were dry. What had started small was now spreading, and spreading fast.

⚓

"All right," the princess said. "Here's what I want you to do. Rouse the sweeper and the slaves from the cookroom, then all of you leave right away. You'll have to use the service door. Then raise the alarm, and don't stop shouting till you get some help. This fire will destroy the palace if it isn't put out quickly, and many lives could be lost. Do you understand?"

"Yes, my lady. But what about you?"

"Claudia and I will follow in a moment. Oh, for heaven's sake, Leondas, leave me be! Will one of you please take the cat?"

"Of course, my lady."

"Well, don't just stand there. Hurry!"

As soon as they had gone, the princess took Claudia's hand and found that it was trembling. "I'm sorry, my dear, but I need you to help me move the bed again."

"Oh, my lady—there isn't time!"

"We'll do it quickly."

"Your document is safe where it is, and we need

to get out while we can. Truly, my lady, it isn't worth dying for!"

"It's worth everything to me. And if you won't help—"

"Of course I will."

"Then let's go."

They ran into the sleeping chamber and tugged at the heavy bedframe. But, as before, it shifted only a little at a time. Hard as they pulled, it was taking too long. The roar of the fire was much louder now; they could hear the crash of roof beams collapsing. The blaze was spreading with astonishing speed.

"Stop! Now!" Claudia shouted, grabbing her mistress's arm. "This is madness. You cannot be queen of Cortova if you're dead. It may already be too late. But if we can't get out of the compound, we can at least go into the atrium, where there's nothing but sky over our heads."

Claudia had used the word *madness* as a figure of speech, but now she saw that Elizabetta was quite literally lost to reason; she seemed not to comprehend anything at all and was making no effort to move.

"My lady," she said, her voice stern, "I will die with you gladly if it comes to that. But I promised your mother I'd look after you. And I intend to keep that promise if I have to knock you senseless and drag you out myself!"

Just then the wall on the other side of the room cracked apart, showering chunks of plaster onto the floor. Flames darted through the openings and quickly reached the ceiling.

"Now!" Claudia shouted, pulling the princess roughly away from the bed. Elizabetta didn't resist, just followed blindly with a shuffling gait—unbearably slow. Already the fire had reached the doorframe. They had only seconds now. And so, just as the ceiling came down with a sickening crash and a shower of sparks, Claudia shoved her mistress out.

She pushed with such force that the princess went flying like an arrow loosed from a bow—out onto the covered porch, where the roof was now ablaze—one lurching, stumbling step after another, till she reached the safety of the garden, tripped on the brick edging of a flower bed, and fell, striking her head on the stone of the path.

And there she lay, insensible, as walls caved in, and beams fell, and everything around her was destroyed.

❦ 25 ❧

A Very Private Place

THE GUESTS STOOD OUTSIDE their villas gazing in horror at the boiling cloud of black smoke that rose like a violent patch of storm in an otherwise perfect summer sky, and below it, hot and bright, the dancing flames. They were strangely silent for such a crowd of people; but really, anything worth saying was already understood.

Alaric stood apart, heavily protected by his men. His meeting with Gonzalo had been mercifully short, but it could so easily have been otherwise—his third miraculous escape in a little more than a week. Either the king of Westria lived a charmed life, or the fates were determined to kill him but were making a mess of it.

Once Alaric's safety had been assured, Tobias and a contingent of knights had gone to offer their help. But the gate to the inner wall was locked, and the guards were away fighting the fire, so they'd come back again. It was a terrible shame—so many willing hands outside with no way to get in.

Tobias and Molly now stood watching in silence with the others. He had his arm around her and was gripping a little too tight, as if he thought he could press the trembling right out of her. Finally she pulled away and looked up at him. She said, "Tobias?" But there was no sound; she was just mouthing the word. So he leaned down, and she whispered in his ear.

"Tobias," she said again, "there's something I need to tell you."

As she seemed so secretive about it, he asked if it was a private matter, and she nodded. When he asked how private, she said, "Very."

"All right then," he said. "Follow me."

Tobias and the lesser knights had been assigned to a former barracks, which at some point in the distant past had been turned into a guesthouse. Unlike the other villas, it was long and narrow, not built in a square around a central atrium. Upon entering, Molly and Tobias crossed a hall punctuated by the doors to the sleeping chambers, then came into a large common room where the men spent their leisure time. It was empty now, showing signs of hasty departure: cards abandoned in midgame lying face down on a table; cups of wine that had been set aside unfinished; cloaks and even weapons that had been left behind.

Tobias led her across this room and through a service pantry in the rear, and opened the back door, revealing a long terrace that extended the entire length of the barracks and overlooked the sea. At one end it abutted a watchtower; at the other it was protected by a wall, so the space was completely enclosed.

"I come out here sometimes when I want to be alone," he said, pulling the door shut behind them. "No one else seems to like it—too windy, I guess. So it's just me and the occasional slave pitching slops over the cliff."

With a gentle hand he guided her along the terrace till they were far enough from the door that anyone who might have been listening couldn't have heard a thing.

"All right," he said. "Tell me." But Molly didn't answer. She seemed more interested in looking at the terrace, and not in a curious or admiring way.

Something about it seemed to alarm her. "What is it?" he said. "What's the matter?"

"I've been here before."

"Surely not."

"I saw it in a vision. Twice. The cat was right there, on that railing. Then he jumped off and walked down that strip of grass."

"How odd. What do you think it means?"

"I have no idea. But I don't much like it."

"Shall we go somewhere else to talk?"

"No. I'll just be quick."

She took a deep breath. He waited.

"You know I was playing chess with the princess just minutes before the fire started."

"Yes. And everything was normal when you left?"

"There was certainly no fire, and I didn't smell any smoke. But there *was* something odd. I ran into Prince Castor as I was on my way out. He'd been spying on us; and when he saw that I was coming, he ran away. Only, I caught up with him."

"And?"

"He turned on me with this horrible, malevolent look that was positively frightening. Then he stood in front of me, like this, to keep me from leaving. There's something very wrong with that child."

Tobias nodded. One couldn't help but notice how spoiled and immature he was.

"He had his hands behind his back, and at first I assumed he was hiding something he'd stolen from his sister. But now I think it must have been a flint and steel. Tobias, I believe Castor set the fire."

He was genuinely shocked. "That's a very heavy and dangerous accusation. I beg you not to repeat it to anyone else. It's Cortova's private business. You really don't want to get involved."

"But what about the princess? She might have died in there."

"If so, then it would be a terrible tragedy—but still none of your business."

She broke away from Tobias then and went to lean on the railing. Suddenly she recoiled and backed away.

"It *is* rather alarming," Tobias said. "Such a long way down."

"Yes," she said, shuddering. "It makes me allover cold with dread."

"Then come over here."

He found a spot that was clear of bird droppings and blown debris. There they sat with their backs against the wall. Molly wrapped her arms around her knees to keep her skirts from flying up. Tobias sat in exactly the same way. They were like a pair of bookends, except that everything about Tobias was larger and longer.

"All right," he said, "let's suppose you're right. Why would Castor do such a thing? He stands to inherit that palace someday. Why would he burn it down?"

"I doubt he's capable of thinking that far ahead, and he probably didn't know it would spread so fast. But he had to be aware that it would put his sister in grave danger. I think that was his intention."

"Do you mean to say he was trying to kill her?"

She paused. Finally, "Yes, I do. And he was quite gleeful about it. When I got to the gate and turned around, he grinned at me like, 'Ha-ha, I'm going to get you! Just you wait and see!' I felt I was being threatened."

When she saw the alarm cross Tobias's face, she said, "What?" But he was already wrapping his arms around her, holding her close. She could hear his heaving breath.

"For pity's sake, Tobias, *what*?"

Now he was stroking her hair and still not saying anything, and it was making her wild with fear. She was just about to scream when he released her, and she saw there were actually tears brimming in his eyes.

"What?" she said again, but softly this time, because she wasn't sure she wanted to know.

"He set the fire, and he's going to blame it on you."

She was stunned. How was it she hadn't thought of that?

"It started right after you left. He'll say he saw you going out, and . . . who knows what lies he'll dream up: you were cackling with glee; you were carrying a torch. . . ."

"But why would anyone believe such a thing? It doesn't make any sense."

"Oh, Molly—why do you think?"

After that they sat in silence, thinking parallel thoughts.

"What's the chance," he said, "that we could go directly to the stables, and collect our horses, and get out of here right now—before he has a chance to accuse you?"

"No, Tobias. Forget it. It would be like an admission of guilt if I ran away like that, and Gonzalo would send an army thundering after us."

"He'll have to put the fire out first. That should give us some time."

"Not enough."

"Then, is there anything *else* you can do?" He said it slowly and meaningfully, and she understood what he meant: Could she somehow use her Gift to—what? Turn back time so she could stop the fire before it happened? Strike Prince Castor dumb so he couldn't spread false tales? Float up in the air and fly back to Westria?

"It doesn't work that way," she said. "I wish—"

But she never got to say what it was she wished, because just then the door to the guesthouse opened and a swarm of soldiers poured out. They wore the black and gold of the army of Cortova, and their swords were already drawn.

They'd come for her with astonishing haste.

Molly and Tobias put up a fight, but no amount of screaming, kicking, and biting could save them in the end. Two men carried Molly away, like workmen hauling off a carpet, leaving Tobias prostrate on the terrace with five more holding him down.

After a while Tobias realized that struggling wasn't just a waste of effort, it was actually making things worse. So he stopped, lay as motionless as he could, and waited. Finally, when the soldiers seemed to have calmed down a bit, he said in his most reasonable voice, "I don't understand what just happened. Why have you taken the lady away?"

"She's under arrest by order of the king," said one of the guards.

"On what charge?"

"Arson. And murder."

"But she never—"

"Keep your mouth shut, boy, or we'll arrest you as well."

The fact that he wasn't *already* arrested came as a pleasant surprise. It meant that if he behaved himself, eventually they'd let him go. Then somehow he'd find a way to set Molly free.

But for now he lay unmoving, his cheek pressed hard against stone, a large man sitting heavily on his back, and nothing to look at but a lot of hobnailed boots and the pointy ends of swords. And beyond all that, a railing, and the sea.

Part Five

Endgame—the final phase of the game.
The endgame generally starts after queens have
been exchanged or when the immediate goal
is to promote a pawn.

Sacrifice—the voluntary offering of one of a player's
pieces in exchange for a favorable advantage.

Poisoned pawn—a pawn that, if captured, would
create a serious disadvantage to the capturing side.

Counterattack—the launch of an attack by
the defender.

Capture—moving a piece to a square occupied by
an enemy piece, thereby removing the enemy
piece from the board.
Once a piece is captured, it may never
return to the game.

Day Fourteen

❦ 26 ❧

A Favor

THE NOTE HAD COME from the royal physician, not from the princess herself. Marcus thought this a bad sign. In the past she'd always written to him in her own hand, however brief the message might be. Was she too injured even to pick up a pen? He could only guess. No one outside the family had been allowed to see her till now. And the one public announcement had been brief: the princess had survived the fire and was expected to live. But that could mean almost anything.

They'd moved her to the queen's old chambers, her own rooms having been completely destroyed, and

Marcus was worried about this.

On their ride back from Westria, Betta had talked a lot about her mother—especially their final hours together, which had naturally made a strong impression. She'd described the scene, still vivid in her memory all these years later: the dim candlelight; the dark, stuffy room; and everyone so grim and silent. She'd described her own feelings, too: how frightened and confused she'd been, and how she hadn't been able to understand why her mother had to *leave* and where exactly she was going.

Now, to put the princess in that very same room—well, it seemed unwise. Marcus just hoped she wouldn't so much dwell on her mother's death as remember the living woman she'd loved so dearly. To lie where her mother had lain, to touch the things she had touched—who could tell? Maybe it would actually give her comfort.

❧ ❦

The physician met him in the anteroom.

"Thank you for coming, my lord Marcus. Her Highness has been most anxious to speak with you. I confess I put it off till now because I didn't think she was strong enough to have visitors. But she was so insistent that I thought perhaps it would ease her mind if you came. That's the only reason I'm allowing it."

"I understand. May I see her now?"

"In a moment. First let me mention a few things."

"Of course."

"She made her way out into the atrium, which saved her life. But apparently she tripped in her haste, suffering a severe blow to the head; she was unconscious when we found her. Moreover, when the colonnade collapsed, a beam crushed her foot. She may never walk on it again. The burns on her legs are severe, and flying sparks fell on her arms and her face. There will be scars. And as you would expect, the smoke has affected her lungs. But it's her legs and the burns that concern me most. Infection, you know."

Marcus nodded. So far it was actually better than he'd feared.

"She's highly agitated. She keeps calling for you and for Claudia, her servant." He paused for a moment. "As Claudia died in the fire, I now turn to you."

"Does she know about Claudia?"

"She does not, and I am keeping it from her. Apparently the woman was of special importance to her."

"What shall I say if she asks? I have never lied to her. Perhaps that's why she trusts me as she does."

"I'll leave it to your best judgment. If you must tell her, then do it gently."

"I will. Anything else?" He could hear Betta coughing from the next room.

"The girl from Westria, Lady Marguerite. It was she who apparently started the fire."

"I've heard that. But it must be a mistake. The princess was especially fond of her; she told me so herself. And what would the girl hope to gain?"

"That's not for either of us to decide. What matters is that the princess doesn't know. Perhaps you can avoid mentioning it."

"All right."

"That's all, then. Go ahead. But please be brief and don't tire her out."

⚶

The room was dark, just as she'd described it from that day long ago. The windows had all been shuttered, and there was no other light besides the candles on the tables by the bed. The air was overwarm and musty from long disuse. It smelled, besides, of medicine and sweat. And over all that was the pungent odor of burning, which filled every corner of the palace now and would for many months, maybe even years. Marcus was tempted to pull the shutters wide, let in some light and air. But he didn't. The physician must have his reasons.

Betta lay under a linen bedsheet, the coverlet

having been removed. The weight of it would be painful, he thought, pressing against her burns and other wounds. Her head and chest had been propped up on pillows.

"My lady," he whispered as he approached the bed. "It's Marcus here."

She looked up at him with a kind of feverish excitement and tried to speak. But that started her coughing, and she couldn't stop, so she covered her mouth with one hand and reached out to him with the other. He took her hand and held it gently in both of his. He saw the bandages on her wrist and arm.

"You came!" she finally said. "I'm so glad."

She was breathing rapidly, almost panting. *She's not getting enough air,* he thought, resolving to speak to the physician about the shutters.

"I will always come when you want me."

"I've been calling for weeks, and nobody would listen."

"No, my lady, you are mistaken. It's only been one day."

"Has it really?"

"Yes."

"It seems like forever. Marcus, there is something I need you to do for me. It's very important. Will you promise?"

"Of course, if it's within my power."

"It is. Sit, please. It's hard for me to look up at you."

"All right." He released her hand and brought a chair over to her bedside. "Now what would you have me do?"

"Go to my bedchamber—"

"Oh, my lady! It's—"

"I know, it's a ruin. I'm not *that* addled. But there is something hidden there. Chances are it will have survived. And I must have it, Marcus. You must get it for me. It will ease my mind to know that it is safe."

"I will try."

"Find Claudia—my old servant, you know her. She'll show you where it is. You'll have to move the bedframe, and it's heavy; but that'll be nothing to you. It's under a loose tile, in the corner."

"I might not be allowed to go there, my lady."

"I'll write something out, giving you permission. And you must go alone—except for Claudia, of course. This is very private business and of great consequence. I'm very afraid that when the workmen start clearing out the rubble, they'll stumble across it by accident. You have to get there first."

"I'll go today. But can you tell me more—what it is I'm looking for and where exactly it's hidden?"

"Claudia will show you. She knows everything."

There was no help for it. "My lady, you will have to tell me yourself. I cannot ask Claudia."

She looked at him, then, with such alarm and sorrow on her face that it made him long to lift her and hold her like a little child. But he couldn't do that. He could only wait for her to ask.

"She died in the fire, didn't she?"

"Yes, my lady."

"I don't remember. I don't remember anything."

"That's probably for the best."

She turned her face away, and he could hear her weeping. The sobs soon turned into loud, spasmodic coughs, and the physician came hurrying into the room. He went to the other side of the bed and felt the princess's pulse.

"Perhaps no more company for today," he said, giving Marcus a significant look. "Maybe he can come back tomorrow, when you are feeling stronger."

"No," Elizabetta said. And though her voice was hoarse and rough, she sounded astonishingly regal. "He will leave when I am ready for him to leave. And now we would like to be alone."

The physician was startled by this, but he gave her a low bow and backed out of the room. When the door had shut with a delicate click, she reached again for Marcus's hand.

"I'm glad it was you who told me."

He just nodded.

"She was like a second mother, you know. I loved her very much."

He nodded again.

"She would have died for me, Marcus; I'm sure of that. And though I can't remember what happened, I wouldn't be surprised if that's exactly what she did."

"If so, then she is with the saints and angels now."

"She would be in any case."

He gave her silence, and she took it. When she was ready, she said, "It's a document bearing the king's seal. It's in a metal case, hidden under a tile in the floor. Near the corner, under the bed."

"I should be able to find it."

"Wrap it in something or hide it under your clothes. I don't want anyone to see it or even to know that it exists. Then bring it to me, just to put my mind at rest. After that, I'm afraid I must beg another favor."

"All right."

"Keep it for me, somewhere secret."

"I will do that gladly, my lady. Your document will be safe. No one shall see it or find it accidentally. And no one will know I have it."

"Good."

"Can I assume you will want it back at some point?"

"You are as sharp-witted as ever, dear Marcus. Yes, I will want it back—at the time of my father's death."

He just barely stifled a gasp—because suddenly he knew exactly what that document must be. It explained why she'd been so eager to learn about statecraft, and politics, and the history of Cortova.

"Your face is flushed of a sudden," she said.

"I was just thinking," he replied.

"May I be privy to your thoughts?"

He took a chance.

"I was thinking how splendidly you will rule Cortova."

⫷ 27 ⫸

A Child Has Eyes,
Same as Anyone

"YOUR MAJESTY," ALARIC SAID, barely keeping his voice under control, "I demand to know why you have arrested one of my subjects—and a particular friend of mine, as you are perfectly aware. I would also know why you have refused to see me till now. It is altogether an outrage and a grave discourtesy."

Gonzalo met Alaric's ice with fire. "I had more important things to worry about than your dignity and your feelings. My palace was burning. My daughter almost died. And your 'particular friend' was the cause of it all. She may be one of your subjects; but she's in my kingdom now, and she shall pay for what she did, as any criminal must."

They were standing in the middle of the room, eye to eye, but they were not alone. Alaric had brought twenty of his knights; Gonzalo had many more.

"On what possible grounds do you accuse the lady of such a heinous crime?"

"There was an eyewitness."

"Are you telling me that someone actually *saw* her set the fire?"

"I am."

"And may I know who that person might be?"

Gonzalo lifted his head defiantly and looked down his nose at Alaric. "Yes," he said. "It was my son, Prince Castor."

Alaric was speechless for a moment, his mind racing. "But he's just a child," he finally said, knowing that sounded hopelessly feeble.

"He has eyes, same as anyone."

"Then he must have been mistaken."

"He was not. Castor was very clear about what he saw."

"If so, then why didn't he stop her, or go for help, or warn his sister of the danger?"

"Are you calling my son a liar?"

"I suppose I am."

"Then you will pack up your things and be gone

from here before the sun has set."

"I would do so gladly, but I will not leave without the lady Marguerite. She's been falsely accused and is being wrongfully held. Perhaps you ought to question your son a little more closely, find out what really happened."

Gonzalo's knights were moving in now, and Alaric saw that in his fury he'd gone too far—and in doing so he'd shut a door that he very much needed to keep open.

"Forgive me, Your Majesty," he said. "In my agitation I quite forgot myself. I only ask that the lady be tried in a fair and judicious manner, that she be well treated until her guilt or innocence has been judged, and that she be allowed to have visitors and advisers in her cause."

A glimmer of triumph sparkled in Gonzalo's eyes. Alaric watched him enjoy his little moment. "You may remain until her fate is decided," Gonzalo said. "Then you will leave Cortova and never return. There will be no alliance and no marriage."

"I want to speak with the lady myself. I want to be assured that she is well treated."

"You may *want* those things, Alaric, but you will not have them. This is my kingdom, not yours. Already I am letting you stay when you are no longer welcome.

Don't ask for anything more." And then when the king of Westria showed no indication of leaving, "This conversation is over."

As Alaric was on his way out and had almost reached the door, Gonzalo spoke to his men in a carrying voice, clearly intending for him to hear: "Back in Westria, you know, they say she's a witch."

～✦ ✦～

Tobias and the king stood side by side on the terrace where Gonzalo's men had come for Molly. Only this time the common room was well guarded by Alaric's knights, as was the south wall, though it was of such a height that you'd need a ladder to scale it.

"So from the beginning," said the king. "Why were you here?"

"Molly had something important to say, and she didn't want to be overheard. This seemed a private place."

"Both private and remote. So how did they find her?"

Tobias considered. "I'm just guessing, but maybe one of Gonzalo's men—disguised somehow, most likely as a slave—asked around for her, and someone remembered seeing us go off in the direction of the villa. It's no secret that I often come out here. Knowing that, the rest would be easy. The villa was empty. Even the slaves were outside, gaping at the fire. And I know for a fact that the door wasn't locked."

Alaric nodded.

"They seemed quite prepared. They knew I was with her—well, I suppose they would since we left together—and they took that into account, in case I might be a problem—"

"The young Goliath."

Tobias flushed with anger. "So I was called in jest back when I worked in your stables."

"I'm sorry, Tobias. I didn't mean it that way."

What other way was there? But Tobias set it aside. "It doesn't matter," he said. "The point is that the whole thing was handled quickly and efficiently."

"Were they rough with her?"

"More than they would have been if she hadn't fought so hard. But Molly's tough. A few scrapes and bruises are the least of my concerns."

"Yes," Alaric said. He paced in little circles, thinking, then came back and faced Tobias. "What was the important thing she wanted to tell you?"

Tobias paused, remembering how stunned he'd been when she'd told him her suspicions. "That she ran into Prince Castor as she was leaving the princess's rooms. He was behaving in an odd and suspicious manner. She thinks he's the one who set the fire."

But the king wasn't shocked at all. "I agree with her. *He's* the accuser, you know. Castor will swear in court that he saw Molly do it."

Tobias hardly moved. For a moment he just let it all wash over him. "That's exactly what I was afraid of," he finally said. "It's very bad."

Alaric went over to lean on the railing, looking down at the sea, having his own private moment of despair. It was almost exactly where Molly had stood while she was still safe and free. Tobias remembered how she'd jumped back of a sudden, saying it filled her with dread. And with that memory there came the sudden realization that he might never see her again. He turned away, not wanting Alaric to see the tears that were welling in his eyes.

But the king didn't notice. He was still staring at the sea.

"I suggested to Gonzalo that the prince might have been mistaken, and he took very high offense at that. He'll never believe that his son started the fire and then lied about it. And even if he did, he'd keep the boy's secret anyway and let Molly take the blame. Heir to the throne and all that."

"Yes," Tobias said, sweeping an arm over his face to wipe away the tears.

"Whatever the laws of Cortova might be, if there's an eyewitness, and he happens to be the king's son, I don't see any hope that she'll be fairly tried. I'm not even allowed the courtesy of visiting her or sending someone to advise her during the questioning. As you said so succinctly, it's very bad."

"Then we'll have to free her ourselves."

"Well, if you've got any ideas on how to do that, now would be the time to share them, because I'm completely at a loss. We can't storm the walls without an army, and my army is in Westria, and we haven't the time to bring it here. Gonzalo won't drag this out. The trial will be soon. So whatever we do, we'll have to do it quickly"

"I know."

The word *hopeless* hung in the air, unspoken.

❦ 28 ❧

Tell Me What to Do

SIGRID? I NEED YOU! Right now, *please*!

I'm here, Molly. I've been here all along.

That's good, because any minute now they're going to kill me.

No. I don't think so.

Really? Well, they've locked me up in a hot, dark room with guards outside and just one little window with bars on it, so high on the wall not even Tobias could reach it; and I'm accused of—

I know all that. Remember? I've been here all along.

Then tell me what to do.

Molly, I want you to pay close attention to what I'm

about to say. You won't like it, but it's the truth. And your life depends upon it.

I'm listening.

I don't have the answers. I'm limited in my powers and my knowledge of the world. I'm nothing compared to you. And every time you turn to me for help, you turn away from your own incredible powers. It's up to you to save yourself.

But I don't know how.

Of course you do. You're the Great Seer of Harrowsgode; you possess the Gift of King Magnus. Just be what you are.

Oh, Sigrid!

I'm shutting the door now, precious child. You're on your own.

⚜

That was hard. It was so hard that Molly curled up like a wood louse and lay there for a very long time. She didn't think at all; she just *felt*, and all her feelings were sad and hopeless.

She might have lain like that a good deal longer if she hadn't needed to use the chamber pot. Gradually her mind became aware of this, and the delicate question arose as to whether she should just go ahead and wet herself—and that certainly *was* tempting—or get up and make use of the vessel they'd given her for that purpose. And the more she considered this, the clearer it became how absolutely pathetic she was, lying there feeling sorry for herself and not even *trying* to do anything about it.

So she got up and found the pot, and used it. Then she sat on the floor with her back to the wall and stared at the small patch of sunlight on the floor, focusing her concentration. When she shut her eyes, the patch of light was still there, hovering in the darkness.

Soon the familiar floating sensation began. It was as if she were underwater, weightless and warm. The light had faded now, and there was only darkness. She waited for whatever would come. Her spirit knew what she needed. Molly just had to be patient.

There was no time anymore. It was just now, and more now, and still more now.

Finally, out of the nothingness that spread around her in every direction, there came a sound—more a feeling than a sound, really, just the vibration of it— and at the same time a soft glow of light.

Still she waited.

Here was the cat now, *her* cat, poking around in the ruin of the princess's rooms. As always, he moved daintily for such a large animal, stepping over broken beams, weaving through the wreckage. Here was the cup, the Loving Cup, or what remained of it—crushed and half melted now. Leondas inspected it, then gazed out at Molly. Or that's how it seemed anyway; he was looking out, and she was looking in.

Next he found the chessboard, or rather a corner of it, and a few scattered pieces. All of them were black now. Leondas selected one of them and touched it with his nose. Molly saw that it was a queen. The vision began to fade, and then it was gone.

Dark.

Quiet.

She was floating.

Her mind grew restless; her feelings rose up. She wanted to say, "What bloody use is any of this to me?" But she fought against it. Her spirit would tell her what she needed to know when she needed to know it. Sigrid had said so.

Hard as it was, she must be patient.

She waited.

She heard footsteps outside. They approached, then gradually receded into the distance. Then there was the sound of a door closing and a faraway voice.

But Molly was no longer listening. She was back inside her spirit-self, where it was dark and quiet. After a while a new vision began to emerge from the shadows, and with it came the thunder of hooves on hard-packed ground. Once again she saw Leondas, but now he was in a forest, just off the path, where weeds and scrub grew in a rich carpet of leaf mulch. He was stalking, as cats do, but his prey was neither field mouse nor bird; he was creeping up on a man.

It was the assassin. Molly didn't know him by face, but she recognized the caped hood of forest green he wore. This was one of Gonzalo's huntsmen. She watched him wait, carefully hidden behind a hawthorn bush, his bow and arrow at the ready. Now Alaric came riding into view. The huntsman drew his bowstring with a strong arm and practiced grace and let the arrow fly. It soared through the air, perfectly aimed, sure to hit its mark—but then, quite unaccountably, the shaft began to bend into the shape of a sickle. . . .

It all happened as it had in real life. Nothing was changed or new—except that she had seen the archer. That was the reason her spirit had sent her this particular vision. That was the thing she needed to know: that it had not been Reynard's man, but Gonzalo's.

Fiercely as she tried to keep her concentration, she gasped at this revelation and couldn't help asking herself why King Gonzalo, of all people, should want Alaric dead. Wouldn't that spoil his little game of playing one cousin against the other?

No, she suddenly realized; it would make things even better. Reynard would inherit Alaric's kingdom, making him twice as rich, with twice as much land and a most formidable army. Gonzalo needn't choose between Westria and Austlind—he could have them both in the form of a single, stronger ally unencumbered by threat of invasion by its neighbor.

And if Reynard thought he could walk away from the alliance with Cortova, then a little blackmail would quickly change his mind—for the world would accept whatever version of Alaric's death Gonzalo chose to tell. So if they came to an agreement on Gonzalo's terms—the very ones to which Reynard had already signed his name—then the king of Cortova would swear it had been an accident.

Molly had entirely lost her focus now, but she knew she could find it again. And she was just about to begin when she heard a clank, then a rattle, as the door to her cell was unbolted and unlocked. When it swung open, there was such a press of soldiers filling the doorway that she could see nothing else but the sky above their heads. Terror passed over her, and then it was gone, replaced by determination. She leaped to her feet, poised and ready to fight.

But fighting wasn't called for, it seemed. The man in front simply leaned down and set a small wooden bowl on the floor. Then he stepped back, shut the door again, and shot the bolt.

It pleased her enormously that they considered her such a threat that they'd brought a whole pack of soldiers just to deliver her bowl of bread—or slops, or porridge, or whatever it was she had no intention of eating. She smiled and sent a loving message of thanks to Sigrid—who was listening, Molly had no doubt—then she sat against the wall again and prepared herself for more.

It was easier this time. She slid almost effortlessly into the trancelike state, and her next vision came quickly.

For once the cat was not in evidence. Molly didn't allow herself to wonder why. Nor did she react when she recognized the setting: the long terrace that ran behind the former barracks where she'd been seized by Gonzalo's soldiers. She fought to keep her concentration, to hold the vision, as Alaric and Tobias came out of the villa and stood together, talking.

She heard every syllable of every word they spoke and followed them, step by painful step, as they moved toward their grim conclusion. And it was devastating, not because they said aloud the things she already knew: that she would die, probably soon, and there was no way they could save her. No, the devastating part was watching the two people she most loved in the world—so close, so lifelike, yet beyond her reach—and knowing she would never see them again.

That was, by far, the hardest thing of all. Beheading (or hanging, or burning at the stake, or however it was they executed criminals in Cortova) would hurt for a moment and then it would hurt no more. But to leave Alaric and Tobias forever was simply past bearing.

This terrible knowledge should have drowned her in another wave of grief, breaking her concentration and sending her back to her former state of hopeless despair. But it didn't. Molly and her spirit were as one now.

All these years, she'd stood in the doorway of the place where her power and wisdom dwelt, taking the occasional cautious step across the threshold, grabbing something, then stepping back and running away. Now she'd entered the room and closed the door behind her—and once inside she was forever changed. She could grieve and watch at the same time; she was patient yet ready to pounce. All would work itself out according to the fates, and if her own death was written in the stars—she *had* been warned!—then she was prepared to accept it. But there was still something that had to be done, and her spirit would guide her. When that mission was clear, she would summon everything burning within her and accomplish this final task.

She sat, unmoving, hardly breathing, as if she'd

been carved from a block of stone. Her thoughts and emotions floated above her; she could practically reach up and touch them. But they did not distract her. She was keeping watch, all her senses primed, for what her spirit would show her next.

"One of the slaves might get inside," Tobias was saying. "Maybe we could send a message—"

"To whom? Who inside the walls would help us?"

"The princess. She can't possibly believe Molly is guilty. They were friends. And she of all people has the power to make Gonzalo see reason."

"That's good, Tobias. A very real possibility. But the princess was badly injured in the fire. She might not be well enough to help."

Behind them, the door from the common room opened—so quietly that any sound it made was swallowed by the wind—and a man slipped out, closing the door again behind him. He was dressed as a slave, but he wasn't there to toss out slops. He was the perfect assassin: powerful, skilled, and as graceful as a dancer, not a single movement wasted or ill considered. A good actor, too, for he had fooled the king's knights. Now he crept forward, as silent as a cat, his sword raised and ready to strike.

Tobias saw him first and cried warning; Alaric wheeled around and ducked under the slashing blade.

Molly could hear the singing of steel against air. She saw Alaric lose his balance and fall. She watched as the man raised his arm to strike again.

But Tobias, large though he was, had always been quick. Now he threw himself between the killer and his prey. And as the sword came down, he caught the underside of the assassin's arm, unbalancing him and spoiling his swing.

Alaric scrambled to his feet and drew his dagger. But Tobias and the assassin were now locked in a brutal embrace, spinning and stumbling, so that it was impossible to strike the one without risking the other.

And something else. The swing Tobias had interrupted had struck him on the shoulder instead. Now his blood was pulsing out in great, sharp jets, splattering the walls and pooling on the stone floor, which soon became slippery with gore. And strong though he was, Tobias couldn't go on much longer.

"Run!" he kept shouting to Alaric. "Go!"

But the king remained, dancing around them with his dagger, trying to catch the assassin as he swung by without doing any more harm to Tobias. Once or twice he succeeded, but never to much effect.

Tobias's movements were becoming erratic now. He was losing his grip on the man's arms, and time was running out. He knew his wound was mortal; and once he collapsed, Alaric (who *wouldn't* save himself, the bloody, stubborn fool!) would be the next to die.

But there was one thing he could still do, and it wouldn't take three seconds. Tobias was a full two stones heavier than the nimble assassin; the weight of his body was his one remaining weapon.

And so—still holding on with the rag-ends of his strength, still skidding on the slick, wet stone—Tobias spun around so that he faced the sea. Then he fell, and the man fell with him—over the marble railing, onto the grassy verge, then over the cliff and down, down, down the sickening drop to the rocks and the sea far below.

❧ 29 ❧

Leondas

FROM A SMALL, LOCKED cubicle within the palace grounds and, beyond the wall, from a terrace that overlooked the sea, two voices joined in a single cry of unspeakable pain. Alaric was on his knees in a pool of blood, his face distorted with rage. And Molly, still frozen, still held within the secret chamber of her spirit, screamed not with her voice, but with her soul.

And still her spirit wouldn't release her, because it wasn't over yet.

Molly watched as the king remained as he was: kneeling alone on the terrace, staring accusingly at the sky, his dagger lying useless on the ground, so heartsick and angry that he'd lost all caution or care for his own safety. She heard from within the villa, as Alaric apparently did not, a riot of clashing swords and grunting men, the thud of bodies falling, and the crash as furniture and crockery were overturned in the melee. Gonzalo's men had overwhelmed Alaric's guard. And the terrace, which had seemed a safe refuge, had become a trap.

The dark foreboding of loss and death that had hovered over her these past weeks now all but swallowed her up. But she struggled against it—not because she really thought she could save the king, but because she was so *very angry* that the fates should be that cruel and because there was something inside her that was growing and boiling till she thought she would burst apart.

It was then that Leondas came into her vision. He was running along the grassy verge at the edge of the cliff, then he darted between the columns of the railing and went to Alaric's side. The cat rose on his hind legs, pawing the king's chest, trying to get his attention but only succeeding in spotting his doublet with Tobias's blood. He let out a plaintive cat-yowl, loud and insistent. The fur rose up on his back with fright. He yowled again.

Molly felt his fear and cried his cries. She touched Alaric with her cat's paws.

Now they were streaming through the door, others coming up a ladder and over the far wall—three men, five, seven, ten, then more than she could count. In the space of three heartbeats, it would be over. There would be no escape except the one Tobias had already taken.

Molly felt a charge coursing through her body then, as if she'd been struck by lightning. And for a moment it filled her with its fire so that her skin was alive with the heat of it and every hair on her body rose up in alarm. The floor beneath her began to tremble. Her scream became the howl of tempest-winds as she felt all that power flowing back out of her, like some unstoppable force of nature. And in her vision Leondas began to grow and change. He was taller than a man, then taller than the building, and still he grew. His teeth were long and sharp like daggers, his vicious claws bared, and his eyes blazed red with menace: he had become the form of Molly's rage, a monster of retribution.

Gonzalo's soldiers froze—those who hadn't the power or the wit to run away—as Leondas cupped them with his blood-soaked paws and flung them, two or three at a time, over the edge of the cliff. Then he took the king of Westria gently in his mouth, as mother cats carry their kittens, and bore him over the wall to safety.

He stepped carefully over the bodies of Alaric's

fallen men. Molly saw Lord Brochton lying among them and forgave him in passing, thanking him for dying in the service of his king. On Leondas went, away from the bloody barracks in the direction of Alaric's villa.

Those of Alaric's men who hadn't been assigned to guard the villa had been roused by the sounds of battle. Now they were racing toward the terrace, unaware that it was already too late. Then they saw Leondas with Alaric in his mouth, and they actually dared to challenge him. They had to know that such a monster could not be slain with swords, but these were men whom Alaric had chosen for their loyalty and their courage—and like Tobias and Heptor Brochton, they would die trying to save him.

But to their astonishment, Leondas laid the king gently down and turned away. As they watched, stunned, he seemed to grow even more enormous, his graceful cat-steps causing the ground to tremble as he went: through the trees toward the inner curtain wall—built a thousand years before and reinforced many times since—and pulled it down with the swipe of a single paw.

Leondas knew where he was going. He made his way judiciously, not wishing to do unwarranted harm—past screaming people, stepping easily over buildings—until he'd reached the council chamber. There he crouched, and with his nose he pushed in the door and broke away a section of the wall and the roof above it.

Gonzalo had heard the screaming outside and had retreated to the far side of the room, his guards massed in front to protect him. But the cat pushed them aside. They were nothing to him, just soldiers doing their duty. It was Gonzalo he wanted.

Leondas took the king of Cortova in his claws, then squeezed him hard as he pulled him, screaming, out of the council chamber—where he'd played his ugly little games and hatched his evil plans, which had taken the lives of so many valiant men—and popped him into his mouth and bit down hard.

Then he swallowed.

And it was over.

Molly's rage was spent. She felt it go, and it was as if a cool breeze was blowing across her. She opened her eyes and saw the dust motes dancing in the small ray of light that streamed in from the high, barred window. She looked down at her hands, touching the left with the right, turning the gold ring on her finger and thinking of Tobias. Then she did something quite ordinary and natural.

She wept.

Part Six

Critical move—a move that should be
played carefully and slowly.
Critical moves often include complicated
decisions, trading pieces, or inflexible plans
that cannot be changed.

Draw—a game that ends in a tie.

Promotion—when a pawn reaches the final rank,
it can be turned into another piece, usually a queen.
Also known as "queening."

Day Eighteen

30

The Queen of Cortova

THE FURNISHINGS HAD BEEN removed from the king's reception room—the chair in which Gonzalo had sat over his breakfast, only a few weeks before, and informed his daughter that two suitors would soon be arriving, and the table where, not long thereafter, he'd written out the change of succession. Now it was empty except for the throne, which had been rescued from the ruin of the council chamber.

There Elizabetta now sat, dressed in a simple chiton of cream-colored linen. It had been hastily made—all her clothes having been destroyed in the fire—according to her precise stipulations: that the fabric was to be plain and that the sleeves should be long enough to cover the bandages on her arms. She had compromised on the gold fibulae. Estella had reminded her that she was the queen now and she really ought to look like one, and Elizabetta had granted her the point. But they were the only ornaments she wore. There was not even a crown to be had, except her father's, and that she'd refused to touch.

She looked out at the assembly before her. Alaric stood on one side of the room with his remaining knights and his ladies. This included Molly, who looked more like an invalid than Elizabetta did. On the other side stood Reynard and his son with an equal number of knights to those that Alaric had brought. With the addition of the queen's own men, the room was very crowded.

"I thank you all," she began, "for remaining here till I was well enough to meet with you. And I apologize— though no apology could possibly suffice—for what you have borne at my father's hand. If you now wish to leave this place where you have known such terrible loss and suffered such indignities, I will certainly understand. But I hope, instead, you will stay and help me build something new and hopeful out of the wreckage of my palace, and my kingdom, and these negotiations."

There was the soft hum of assent. Acknowledgment

and apology wouldn't bring back the dead; but the words still needed to be spoken, and no one doubted she'd meant them sincerely.

"My lord king Reynard and my lord king Alaric, I will be honest with you, as my father never was. Cortova is under attack by enemies who threaten our trade in the Southern Sea. These past few years we have emptied our treasury building ships and manning them, hoping to pull the prize back out of the fire. The luxury you saw here was just a brave show meant to lure you in, to trick you into an alliance in which you would pay far more than you would gain."

The soft hum had grown to whispers and growls, but there remained a willingness to hear her out, if only because at last someone was telling them the truth. She had counted on that and was glad she'd been right.

"But I have a very different proposal to make."

She waited. The room grew still.

"Our true wealth is the same as it ever was: our coastline, ports, and shipyards; our expert seamen, fine roads, and system of banking. And we have far more ships now, many of them new, than we ever had before. We are like the farmer whose fields are rich and well tilled, in a land where the sun is bright and the rain dependable; all he lacks is the money to buy seed."

She had their attention now. She folded her hands, doing her best to look regal, and succeeding at it quite well.

"What if we bond together, our three kingdoms? Think of us as partners in a business. You help Cortova fight the Frasians, and in return you will each take a portion of all we earn in trade."

The room burst into sudden conversation. She let it go on just long enough, then continued to speak without raising her voice. The people grew quiet again so they could hear.

"I am perfectly aware that you two cousin-kings have been enemies these last two years. My father was aware of it too, and used it against you. I personally think it's a pointless waste. Why not combine our forces and build peace and prosperity instead of sowing hate and distrust?"

"A triple alliance, then?" Alaric asked. "Is that what you propose?"

"Yes. And while I'm being frank and truthful, there is one more thing I must tell you. The document that makes me queen of Cortova bears a stipulation. The change of succession is 'conditional to the signing of a satisfactory treaty of alliance with either the king of Westria or the king of Austlind.' I don't see that a triple alliance is in any way contrary to that requirement. If anything, it's an improvement upon it, and my legal advisers agree that this is so. But to be plain, if there is no alliance, my brother becomes king."

She'd expected an outburst and was rather surprised by the silence that met this confession. Perhaps they were considering Castor on the throne. It was a sobering thought indeed.

"So," she went on, "if you are willing to consider it, we can begin discussing the terms. I will hear your thoughts and needs, and suggest some of my own. We can all prosper if we work together."

"And the marriage?" This from Reynard.

"I am not prepared to discuss the marriage at present. Is that a difficulty?"

"It was meant to seal the bargain."

"Yes. But I cannot marry Rupert and Alaric both. How if I show my sincerity to you, and bind our two kingdoms together in another way?"

"I don't understand what you mean."

"How if I send my brother to be fostered in Austlind, Reynard? He is next in line for the throne after me. Such an offer is generally considered to be a great honor, a mark of special trust. I believe your knights and your master of arms might do wonders for Castor, teach him to be a man of honor—as they did so very nicely with your cousin Alaric."

Reynard flushed with discomfort, but he answered straight. "I will accept that as a mark of special favor," he said. "I am willing to discuss the matter."

"That's all I ask. Now, gentlemen, my physician is most insistent that I rest during the heat of the day. Shall we meet again in the cool of the late afternoon and begin our talks? We can dine here tonight and continue our discussions over the meal. I wish to make a good beginning and follow with all speed, for we have robbed you of enough time already. Is that acceptable to you?"

Both kings nodded assent.

"Thank you," she said. "I will send for you this afternoon."

The room hummed with conversation as the crowd moved toward the door. But her voice floated over the din.

"Excuse me, my lord king Alaric," she said, "but will you stay a moment more?"

Reynard turned on his heel, angry. "What is this? More trickery?"

"Not at all, my lord king of Austlind. I've promised to be fair and openhanded in our dealings and so I intend to be. This has nothing at all to do with the alliance. It's a personal matter, just something I need to say."

❧ 31 ❧

Requiem

MOLLY WAITED IN ALARIC'S villa, as he'd asked her to do. Different knights were staying there now, Lord Brochton and the others having died along with Tobias. And while these new men treated her kindly, they kept their distance. Molly found this a relief. For more than anything, she wanted to be alone just now, unwatched and uninterrupted, in the world of her own private reverie.

It had been almost exactly a year since Alaric had called her back to court and asked her to go to Austlind to find a Loving Cup. It had been early summer, still a little cold and wet in the mornings. They'd walked in the garden, and he'd explained it all to her: his desperate need for an alliance to protect Westria against Reynard and the importance of gaining a proper wife to provide him with an heir. All of this had led to Cortova and the princess, the answer to everything.

So Molly had gone to Austlind and brought back the cup. By then it was late summer or early autumn. After that had come all the planning, the choosing and training of men, the long correspondence with Gonzalo, and the ruse of her betrothal to Tobias. That had taken them through the winter and spring and into another summer, till a year had passed and they were ready to set out—with nothing unconsidered, every preparation made, and perhaps a little too much confidence in their ultimate success.

Looking back on that now—if she waved away all they had suffered and all they had lost, which was a very hard thing to do—Molly saw that indeed they had gotten what they'd come for. Elizabetta was, even now, declaring her love to Alaric, a love so deep it could never be altered, a love he shared, a love Molly herself had brought into being. And truly, it would be hard to find him a better queen, for Betta was wise and kind as well as beautiful. As for the alliance, they now stood to gain something much better than a treaty against Reynard: true peace and amity on the continent, with prosperity thrown in.

If only it hadn't come at such a terrible price.

She studied her hand and played with the ring, thinking about Tobias. She remembered him as a boy, so long ago, darting in to catch the priceless goblet she had dropped, the first of many times he'd saved her skin.

Oh, by all that was sacred, *why did the fates have to choose Tobias*? Was there no justice in the world? He'd never done a mean or a cowardly thing in his life. Not one. He had the soul of a saint and the heart of a lion.

Tears were streaming down her face now; she couldn't help it. She felt emptied out, incomplete, because he would never come ambling into her sight again with that sweet smile of his and that graceful way he moved, his thoughts of nothing but what *she* needed or wanted and how he could help her. She would never again catch him watching her or see him blush and turn away. They'd never laugh again at their own private jokes that no one else understood.

How many times had she said of Tobias that he was always there when she needed him? Well, he wouldn't be there anymore, and she felt strangely angry that he should desert her now, though she knew perfectly well he would have lived if he could. But oh, she couldn't bear it. She couldn't; she couldn't!

She couldn't.

She touched the ring again—as she would many times, every day that followed, for the rest of her life—and mourned Tobias, wholly and properly. She blessed him and sent her love to him as she never had while he still lived—because she just figured he understood and didn't need to be told—and promised to remember everything he'd taught her and everything they'd done together, for as long as she lived, and to be worthy of having had such a friend.

❦ 32 ❧

It Was Really
Quite Convenient

THAT'S HOW HE FOUND her, red-faced and weeping, alone in the sitting room. His men had been standing discreetly at a distance, and that had been the right thing to do. All the same, it broke his heart that she should have been so very alone with such a mountain of grief.

"You're back," she said, wiping her face.

"As you see." He offered his hand and helped her up. "Come," he said, "I have news for you."

"Good news, I hope."

"Very good. We'll go to my room. There are far too many eyes here, and we must talk in earnest." He led her to his chamber and asked that they not be disturbed. "Now sit, and I shall tell you."

He seemed almost feverish with excitement. She'd seen him this way a few times before, and it had dazzled her then. But since he'd become king and the weight of the world had fallen on his shoulders, he'd become more solemn and walked with a heavier gait.

"The princess?" she said, helping him along. "What had she to say?"

"That she thinks very highly of you, considers you a friend, and is painfully aware of the terrible pain and loss her family has caused you. She wishes to do something, however small, in recompense. She asked what I thought might please you, that is within her power to give."

"You talked about *me*?"

"Among other things. Now listen. I told her that there's a part of Austlind that is your ancestral home and that you have a very deep attachment to it."

"You didn't mention Harrowsgode?"

"Of course not. I just said that the region was to the north, and it was a wasteland, really, hardly populated at all."

She blinked, not following him exactly but trying.

"She suggested that Reynard might be willing to

exchange this worthless territory for an equal amount of land on the northeast corner of Cortova, which would not only be fit for growing crops but would offer him access to the sea. It's a generous proposal. He's sure to agree."

"And then?"

"Well, obviously Betta will give it to me, I will give it to you, and you will give it to the king of Harrowsgode. Your people will finally have their own kingdom. And as it is not their custom to keep an army, out of reverence for human life, I'll provide troops to patrol the border—for even if everything goes as planned and we are to live in a time of peace, I regret to say there will always be thieves. So what do you say? A pretty neat solution, is it not?"

"It's astonishing, Alaric. Truly. Please tell her that I thank her with all my heart."

"You can do it yourself. I suspect that before these negotiations are over, she'll drag you in for at least one more game of chess."

Molly smiled. "I hope so. I like her very much. She's worthy of you, Alaric, and that's saying a lot. She'll make a splendid queen."

"So she will."

"And Reynard? Do you think he'll agree to this

triple alliance? It doesn't seem altogether fair, even to me, that you should get the princess while he gets Castor!"

He laughed. "Reynard will get everything he needs, and more. And he can find his son another bride."

He got up and went over to the big leather chest in the corner and opened the lid. Then he took out a box and stood with his back to her, holding it in his hands, doing his best to control his breathing. Finally he came and sat beside her again.

"What is that?" she said. She recognized the box, of course, but she couldn't make out what it was doing there and why he was handing it to her.

"You know what it is."

"Really, Alaric, I'm confused."

"Just open it. Don't make a fuss."

She gave him a look, then took off the lid.

"Unwrap it," he said.

"But, Alaric—"

"Please, Molly. Humor me."

"All right." She lifted the bundle out of the box and began to peel off layers of silk—first emerald green, then scarlet, then saffron, then robin's-egg blue, and then the final layer, white as a cloud. And then it was in her hands, the Loving Cup.

"But you gave this to the princess. I saw it in her

room. Then I saw what was left of it in a vision, lying in the ruins of the fire."

"That was a copy. I had it made in Westria before we left."

"I don't understand. You were determined to marry the princess; you believed the fate of Westria depended upon it."

"That's true. And I would have done it too, for all the pain it would have cost me, because I'm the king and my first duty is to my people."

"Then why didn't you use the cup? Why, even before we left for Cortova, did you have a copy made?"

"Because the more I thought about it, the surer I became that it would be wrong to cause her to love me by magic if she couldn't love me for myself—or through that same magic to forget the love I felt for another."

"But I thought, just now . . . the princess . . . I mean, the queen—"

"She loves elsewhere, as do I. It was really quite convenient." His voice grew softer and more solemn. "So, Molly," he said, "will you accept my gift?"

"No," she said, sharp, as if stung. "Indeed, I wonder that you dared to offer it after what you just said. For I, too, am unwilling to love—and be loved—through the powers of enchantment. And I, too, would never, *ever* allow myself to forget the love I already feel, and have felt, and will always feel. . . ."

She put the cup back in its case without even bothering to wrap it. Now she gathered from her lap the many-colored layers of silk and wadded them into the empty space around the stem. "Here," she said, handing the box to the king. "I don't want it."

He took it from her with a face like stone, rose, and went to the trunk in the corner to put it away. Then he returned to his seat like a man on his way to the gallows who is determined to keep his dignity to the end.

"Molly," he said. "I have blundered most terribly. But, you see, I was so overcome with joy at my sudden change of circumstance—that I have been relieved of any obligations to the queen, with no harm to the future of my kingdom, and am now amazingly, unexpectedly, unthinkably free to choose for myself—well, I rather lost my wits, I'm afraid, and didn't think it through.

"Please know that I never meant to compel you to love me through magic: I thought you already did. Giving you the cup was just the impulse of a moment, a grand gesture, my way of acknowledging and celebrating our mutual love, showing you the depth of my commitment. That I failed to consider Tobias in all of this is a mystery, even to me. For a blind man could have seen how much you loved each other. And the fact that— *Oh, God!*"

He buried his face in his hands, and he was trembling.

"The fact that he cannot be here now, asking for your hand, because *he gave his life for mine*, makes my callous assumptions even worse. So I am mortified by what I have done, and I beg you as a friend to forgive me and accept that I meant nothing ill. And if you possibly can, please forget this ever happened."

She reached out and took his hand.

"It's true that I loved—that I still love—Tobias. He was like an essential part of myself: the sweet part, the kind part, the steadfast and brave part. Without him I am incomplete. I will wear his ring for always and think of him every day. He was the best person I ever knew; and though I didn't deserve his devotion, he gave it all the same.

"But the ways of the heart are complicated and not always wise. And I have loved you deeply and for so long that I thought sometimes I might die of it. I've always known that whatever you might feel for me— and yes, I knew you loved me; I just didn't know how much—you would still have to marry someone else. So I've lived with that, and accepted it, and mourned over it since . . . I'm not sure when. I think it was the night Tobias and I came to you in that little village, remember? You were on your way to Dethemere Castle with your makeshift army of common folk armed with nothing but pitchforks and homemade lances. And you were so *alive* with impossible hopes for a moral victory, so bloody eager to lay down your life in your effort to achieve it. And my heart just *ached* with love for you, and admiration, and this terrible fear that you might really die a hero's death.

"I never considered what you might think of me— aside from my being your good-luck charm. But then when we'd finished what we had to say and were about to leave, you sent Tobias out of the cottage so you could speak with me alone. He took that very ill, by the way, though he needn't have since it turned out all you wanted—"

"—was to ask if you had one of your grandfather's Loving Cups, because I needed one to help me win the princess."

"Yes."

"You have such amazing recall for my most unfortunate moments."

"Well, there were so many. I can just take my pick."

Tears sprung into his eyes then. "Shall I tell you when I first began to love you? It will come as a surprise."

"Please. I can hardly wait."

"It was much earlier. We were on the river, with poor Tobias rowing upstream and me half out of my mind with fever, and loss of blood, and that foul elixir Winifred's mother had given me to drink. And you'd hidden me under a canvas or something."

"It was a blanket."

"A blanket, yes, and I was supposed to lie still and impersonate—"

"A cask of herring."

"Exactly. So there I was in the bottom of the skiff, and it was raining, and it was cold, and water was sloshing around; and you peeked under the blanket to check on me. Then you felt my cheek and announced that I was as cold as death."

"You *heard* that?"

"So you sat me up and shook me around like a rag doll. But that didn't seem to have much effect, so Tobias suggested you wrap your arms around me and lay your cheek against mine—to warm me up, you see, and sort of bring me back to life. And you said, 'What if he should wake and find me draped all over him in such a familiar manner?' Then Tobias made a joke about it, and you called him a warty toad."

"Well, it was very ungentlemanly of you to pretend to be asleep all that time."

"I did moan a little. And truly, I was out of my head. But I remember thinking as I lay in your arms that I would gladly stay there forever. And I knew so little about you then, except that you were brave, and smart, and funny, and surprising—and somehow you made every girl I'd ever known seem insipid and bland. You still do."

She looked down at her hands, smiling. "I'm glad you told me that," she said. "And with your permission, I shall remember it always. But it changes nothing. Alaric, a king does not wed his scullery maid, however high he's raised her and however free he is to choose. He must have a suitable consort. I am not, nor could I ever be, that person.

"And thus we have arrived back to where we first began: an unfortunate conversation, best forgotten—apart from the bit I asked permission to remember, of course."

He grinned. "Not really. The princess Elizabetta, soon to be queen of Cortova, has quite captured my imagination. She sets out to rule Cortova, at a particularly difficult time, as the first woman ever to sit upon the Lion Throne. And yet she has chosen—remember that rather handsome, broad-shouldered fellow who stood beside her this morning?"

"I do."

"He's a knight. Wellborn but hardly a prince. Yet she has chosen him to be her consort—because, I would imagine, she trusts him, and loves him, and believes he will help her be a great queen. Imagine that."

Molly tried. It seemed very original.

"Whereas you, Molly, are already far above that knight. You are of noble blood—a direct descendant of King Magnus—and are, moreover, on your own merits, a Magus Mästare, a member of the council, and the Great Seer of Harrowsgode. You have risked your life in the service of Westria and have saved mine on several occasions. I cannot think of a more worthy consort."

"Alaric, you are drawing to a conclusion. Now I beg you to get there with all speed. And speak plain, if you will, so I can understand."

"Very well. I hereby, formally and officially, offer you my hand, my kingdom, and my love. I want you as my queen and the mother of my children. I want you to be the first face I gaze upon in the morning, and I want you by my side as I grow old. Without you I am incomplete.

"So speak plain, Molly: will you have me?"

"Of course I will."

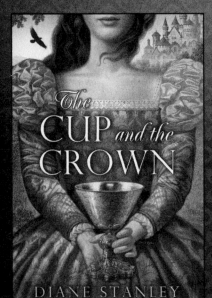